Eaglesworth

a novel by

TR Pearson

Barking Mad Press 2018

D1607793

ONE

1

Sharon
Bishop
2020

1

That house had been sitting empty for years when he rolled into town to claim it. Nobody had spent a night in the place since Frank and Adelaide. They'd come up planning to renovate when Frank got his diagnosis, and they moved back south where all his doctors were.

The estate had a proper name, Eaglesworth, that was spelled out in iron by the road, but big swathes of the original holdings had been parceled off over time. They'd sold the terraced gardens, the boxwood maze, and the patch with the ornamental folly built to look like the Temple of Luxor but in spruce and eight feet high. While the house sat empty, a parade of rascals passed through to pilfer and plunder. They made off with the copper downspouts and most of the conservatory glazing, so when that boy showed up and parked his muddy four by four in the drive, a few of us went ahead and called the law.

They sent Deputy Doby with the neck tattoo. He likes to mix it up with folks, but he didn't stay long and came down disappointed.

"Says it's his," he told us. "Texas tags. Had all the papers and stuff."

Amory at the hardware store was the first civilian to meet him. The boy stopped in because he was overrun with rats, and he suspected if he poisoned them they'd just slink off and stink. Amory sold him traps and glue pads, even stuck him with one of those boxes you plug into a socket. It's supposed to make a high-pitched noise that drives the vermin off, but the one Amory sold the Methodists shorted out and caught on fire, so they got rid of their mice and their fellowship hall both at once.

"What's he like?" we wanted to know.

Amory's not what you'd call expansive. He pulled that face he makes, like he's trying to pass a cue ball. "Forty maybe," he told us. "Had on those boots they wear down there."

We didn't feel like we could just ride up and interrogate the man. We're a nosy lot for sure, but sly and misinformed's our thing, so instead we grabbed the tradesmen he started bringing in for bids, and they told us his name was Rick and he'd come up from Galveston. They said he had a girlfriend who fairly plagued him on the phone and a three-legged cat that slept in the kitchen sink. They thought he was Frank and Adelaide's nephew, or something in the vicinity of it, and they said he talked like he had ambitious plans for that Georgian pile.

We started seeing him out and around in town. He shopped at Dooley's instead of the Kroger, which told us he didn't much care what he ate since Dooley's is a dented can and gristly chuck roast sort of place. Occasionally he'd duck into The Anvil and sit at the bar for a beer and a bump, and a few of us had seen him chatting with red-headed Randi who runs the place.

She'd only tell us, "Turkey and Stella," no matter how we pumped her. Randi's got odd boundaries for a girl who never entirely buttons her shirt.

Truth is, we were nosing around for a legitimate reason. Eaglesworth was about the only antique thing our town had left. Our picturesque timber bandstand had collapsed one fine June day, and our city commissioners had voted to demolish our tobacco shed downtown to make room for a Chrysler showroom and a ladies wear boutique. In the entire county, we had only one historic roadside plaque, and it marked where Longstreet's army had passed while retiring from a rout.

Eaglesworth had been built by an Avent with a turpentine fortune. The cornerstone read 1838. Apparently, he had a homesick Irish bride who was more than a little down on her husband due to his weakness for sherry and his fiery Avent temper. We'd heard his daddy had kicked a man half to death just for wearing his waistcoat wrong.

Our Avent had built that house to help his wife forget about Kinvara, and she even stuck with him for maybe a year or three before she took off with a gardener's assistant. Then our Avent snagged another bride and drove her off as well. Too much sherry. Too much raging around and shooting his guns.

He kept building all along and needed about eight years to finish his house, which had two dumbwaiters and seven chimneys, a banquet hall and a gaming room, a kitchen in the basement that was all bluestone and custom-made iron cookers.

Instead of marrying again, our Avent opted for debauchery, and he organized what our historical society ladies called 'gentlemen's soirees'. He had agents go out and collect women of a certain disposition, and once he felt like they'd raised a quorum, he'd summon all his friends who'd show up to roll around for about a week in the altogether, and after five or six months, that Avent would get an itch and do it again.

He passed away without a proper will, so his brothers down by Roanoke fought over the estate for a while and left the house to sit and rot. Accordingly, it was in rough shape by the time the Crawleys bought it. He was a Crawley anyway. His wife was a Lowell from up east, and they worked 'improvements' that tended to feature marble and gold leaf.

According to the historical society ladies, the Crawley-Lowells played lawn tennis on a court they built behind the house, and they had screaming fights and drank oodles of sloe gin. The wife survived her husband by a pretty considerable stretch, and she lived her last few years in what had been the dining room and kept a man everybody knew as Hudson to see to all her needs. She took in the odd tenant there near the end, and some oldsters around can still recall her sitting out in the yard.

She had one of those high-backed wicker wheelchairs, and Hudson would park her in the sun. Once the shade had found her or she'd grown bored, she'd fire her pistol into the air.

The house sat empty for a while after she passed on, and then Frank and Adelaide came along and bought it. They'd contracted to get the slate roof replaced and have the busted windows all mended when Frank was hit with a couple of light-headed spells and went in for some tests. A scant decade later their nephew or something drove up from Galveston and started making moves like a man who meant to set that mansion right.

We were pleased he'd come, generally speaking, though we had a grumpy outlier or two. Most conspicuously the Gerber brothers who'd long had plans for that estate. Those boys were the local tract home kings. They'd thrown up rancher and faux Tudor suburbs here and there between us and Richmond. They were angling to get into assisted living, and Eaglesworth was their spot.

The historical society ladies wanted Rick from Galveston to donate the property to the county in exchange for a generous write-off. Then they'd raise the funds to fix it up and turn it into a living museum. They seemed to have in mind a Monticello for the turpentine crowd who'd never fought a revolutionary war or penned a constitution but had turned loads of colonial lasses upside down.

Rick from Galveston had other ideas and was free, of course, to do as he pleased while we doubted and second-guessed him and, naturally, ran him down a bit. That's how it went for about eight weeks until Rick's HVAC guy found something. He was down in the kitchen looking to see where he might run a duct when he moved a cupboard, poked through the sheet of gypsum board behind it, and discovered both a spacious hollow and a maple box.

He brought it out of the wall and set it on the soapstone kitchen counter, and his gopher begged him to crack it open because he'd decided there was money inside. That boy was already buying flatboats and fifty-inch TVs when his boss sent him upstairs to fetch down Rick from Galveston.

We know now it was a candle box with a sliding dovetailed lid. Fourteen inches long and five inches wide, just shy of four inches tall, and the whole thing made out of curly maple, even the piece on the bottom nobody much would see. The slots were swollen where the lid went, so it took some prying to work the thing free, but they finally got it mostly off, enough to see what that box was holding — just some sort of dried up nuggets that were rattling around.

Even once they'd spilled them out, they didn't know what they were seeing, until the gopher studied one close enough to tell it was a toe. A little toe. There were seven of them slightly curled and hard.

We've got a sheriff named Glenn, and we dutifully re-elect him every four years. Not because Glenn has any special aptitude for law enforcement, but he's reliable enough and nobody else much wants the job. Glenn personally drove over because, like most of the rest of us, he'd been making do with Eaglesworth gossip and Eaglesworth speculation, and here was a chance to see up close what exactly was going on.

We don't have forensic people, so there was no lab Glenn could carry those little toes to for proper evaluation. Instead, he took pictures of them with his phone and gathered everything into a sack. Then Glenn called the state police in hopes of getting told what to do. They obliged him and had Glenn inform Rick that all his work should stop until they could send somebody out our way to size up the situation.

It took nearly two weeks, but help finally arrived in a filthy Ford Explorer that, underneath the grunge, was a shade of green no sighted human would buy. Various people had gone to the bother to write on the back glass with their fingers. They'd done it in English and Spanish and something probably on the order of teen.

The creature who came out from under the wheel wasn't at all what we'd expected. A doughy white guy in an off-the-rack suit was who we'd been looking for, and instead out popped a large girl with bad hair and metal in her ears. We never found out if she was Inspector Kandy or maybe Detective Kandy. For her part, she'd only show you her badge if you insisted on it, and occasionally she'd remind you she was Kandy with a K.

She had a gun, but she usually left it on the floorboard of her Ford. She wore all her business clothes topside — sweaters and blouses and what looked like men's dress shirts — but you got the feeling the bottom half was the authentic part. Olive drab fatigues. Chippewas. Fuzzy Day-Glo socks. Her Explorer was a rat's nest, and it looked like she'd packed to come by emptying a dresser drawer into a grocery sack.

In the end, we got the sense that Kandy had been less dispatched than banished, that her Richmond bosses had sent her our way because they didn't want her there.

Glenn walked her into the evidence room where that box was up on a shelf, and Kandy pulled out a ballpoint to sort through the giblets and have an introductory scour. Then she followed Glenn up to Eaglesworth where he introduced her to Rick who was itching to start back working on his house.

He'd put a halt to everything inside, but there were some boys in the yard shifting drainpipes until Kandy had a word with Rick and them together, and that word was, "Nope."

She would prove to be more decisive than bossy, and there was nothing terribly high-handed about her. Kandy simply knew what she needed and why and wasn't the sort to circle a thing or dawdle on the fringes, which didn't keep people from getting mad or feeling put upon. Plenty of folks ended up barking at the woman, but Kandy had a badge in one of her pockets and a gun somewhere in her car and wasn't really built for climbing down.

That was something we'd all learn about her, and Rick from Galveston learned it first. He argued and pleaded as he walked Kandy through his house and took her down to the kitchen. He kept at it while showing her the hollow in the wall and the countertop where they'd dumped that candle box.

Rick acquainted her with the problems attached to having his plumbing only half finished while Kandy reached into a cargo pocket and fished out a pair of gloves. They were talced up and lilac colored, and she tugged them on with a pop. Then she pulled out a flashlight and waited on Rick to exhaust his litany.

Once he'd finally quit, Kandy told Rick, "Uh huh. Ok. Yeah," which didn't at all mean she was even remotely persuaded. That was just Kandy's way of commemorating the fact Rick had shut up.

Kandy worked herself into that hollow. She wriggled back between some timbers where the HVAC gopher had nosed around until a snake skin had put him off. Glenn and Rick from Galveston waited for her out in the kitchen where Rick complained in a grumpy whisper to the sheriff for a while. They weren't in a good spot to hear Kandy beyond the racket of her voice.

Glenn stuck his head into the cavity. "You say something?" he asked her. Glenn could see her light beam playing on stuff where stuff had no cause to be.

~~~~~~

At first we couldn't get details in any reliable form because nobody who'd tell us anything was allowed into the house. Deputy Doby said Kandy had found snapshots, but he didn't know of what, and Glenn's girlfriend — Deputy Rachel — said there were definitely photographs, and then she claimed to have further special knowledge she felt she'd best withhold, which we all discounted because Deputy Rachel is a habitual fabricator who claims to know people she's never met and been places she's never gone to, and she routinely insists she only weighs one hundred and fourteen pounds.

We knew Rick from Galveston was powerfully angry because he got full of bourbon at The Anvil one night and put some venom on display. He started out complaining to Randi, but his audience grew with his tab, and soon enough eight or ten of us were hearing all about Rick's monthly nut. He had a house he'd yet to sell in Texas and subcontractors to pay up here, and he was in a spot where he couldn't afford to string his business out.

The more Wild Turkey he had, the more he got down on the HVAC guy and his gopher who could have put their duct work any damn where but ended up in that niche. Soon enough Rick arrived at Kandy like we'd hoped he might.

"Seen her?" he asked us a fair few times, as if we didn't see every damn thing that hit town limits. He ran her down. The way she looked. The way she dressed. The way she talked and acted. Then he knocked back a shot and did his Kandy impression, told all of us, "Nope."

We asked him what she'd found up there, but Rick didn't seem altogether tuned into the details.

"A bunch of pictures, I think," he said. Rick chiefly cared about his stuff. He did take the time and energy, however, to go off on Kandy's hair.

Hers was certainly an odd do for our part of the world, the sort of cut you might see on a fifteen-year-old boy who's spit the bit. There was no hair in places and some hair in others. Plugs of it sticking up and patches of it lying down. It wasn't at all a style that suited a woman the size and girth of Kandy because it seemed to make her big head look even bigger still.

We decided early on Kandy was just a skirmisher Richmond had sent our way. We figured once she'd reported back, they'd dispatch a Frank or a Dave — some guy in a cleaner car with a starched shirt and proper shoes who'd tell us hardly anything, but we wouldn't really care because Frank or Dave was finally in charge.

Kandy took a room at the Laurel Lodge, an old motor inn the highway had bypassed right after a couple from Indiana had sunk their nest egg in it, so the place was about equal parts homey touches and regret. The Laurel Lodge got the Harley clubs that came through because they offered a special rate, so it was Kandy and about a half dozen paunchy guys with sidecars.

Glenn gave Kandy a spot to spread out in the PD annex where they mostly kept all their busted chairs and case files they'd boxed up. She had a sturdy table and a toilet, a big blank wall to tape stuff to, and Kandy imposed a prohibition against all rubberneckers, especially Glenn and Deputy Rachel because Kandy had sussed them out. While we were sniffing, she was sniffing too.

She managed to borrow a helper from Glenn and not the guy we would have picked. He was a civilian employee named

Nathan and we didn't know much about him because he lived a county over, ate his lunch at his desk, and at five o'clock drove straight home.

It's hard to say why Kandy valued him after just brief and spotty exposure, though it could simply have been that Nathan hardly ever talked. He could answer a phone well enough and, apparently, his penmanship was aces, and he could fix the computers in the radio cars even after they'd seemed dead, but he would never just up and freely tell anybody anything.

From her first day with us, Kandy took lunch at the counter in Cuddy's. They claim to serve "homestyle!" food there and, if you grew up in a cold war bunker, it might come pretty close because at Cuddy's they open an awful lot of cans. Kandy seemed partial to the Cuddy version of a cobb salad, which was half a head of iceberg lettuce with random stuff thrown in. We found you could talk to her a little while she was eating, and she'd sometimes even talk back.

She'd discuss her ear studs readily enough and show you her tattoos. Kandy even told Edgar that she'd been conceived by her hippie parents in Sri Lanka and that they'd picked her name off a map.

So she was approachable, but Kandy wasn't terribly forthcoming. Nathan, for his part, was pretty much neither one. We knew they'd found giblets and something beyond them, very possibly snapshots, but we weren't dead sure of anything. That's a hard way to go in a place where folks fuel up on chatter and gossip. We seemed to be right in the middle of something quasi-dastardly, and a couple of our crew tried to get a few details out of Nathan.

We knew the route he took to his Corolla in the evening, and when he passed between the dumpster and the east wall of the post office, some fellows bottled him up and hemmed him in. They didn't jostle Nathan or anything but just asked him about the case. It got back to Kandy who came marching into The Anvil and made her way straight over to us, plopped herself right down.

"Gentlemen," she said. Her bag hit the floor like a depth charge. She had one of those pocketbooks you could haul a couple of hobbits in.

We ordered her a shot of whiskey, and she thanked us and knocked it back.

"Nathan's off limits," she told us. "Nervous stomach. What do you want to know?"

That sounded promising in the moment, but once we'd started in with questions, Kandy turned it all back on us, and pretty soon we were explaining how turpentine gets made.

We brought her up through the Crawley-Lowells to Frank and Adelaide, told her all about the quarreling, the lawn tennis, and sloe gin while we studied Kandy a little. She was a tough one to figure out. Kandy was hulking for a female but still a handsome woman, which she appeared to be fighting every way she could.

"Hear you found something back in a wall up there," we finally got around to saying.

"Uh huh," she told us. "Ok," she said. "Yeah."

Eventually, she asked us about a local murder from eight or ten years ago. A Duggins who'd lived in a ratty old trailer out past the smelting works — which was two crumbling chimneys and a furnace, all of them thick with vines — had been tried and convicted for killing a man, mostly with a hatchet, though he seemed to have grown arm weary and used a wood maul for a while.

We explained that Duggins had been a nut, and not your colorful, interesting sort but more in the way of soured on life and suspicious of everybody. That included the guy he'd ended up killing who was just passing through on a hike.

"The file says he cut off his ears and they found them on the roof of his pump house."

She was making a giblet connection, trying to anyway, but we told her that Duggins had probably never so much as seen Eaglesworth because he'd have to go through town to get there and he flat wouldn't go through town. Too many people out to get him. Too much of a gauntlet to run. That was just the sort of local knowledge we were keen to supply to Kandy. She'd aired a suspicion, and we'd given her chapter and verse on why she was wrong.

Kandy hoisted that handbag of hers off the floor and settled it onto her lap and then rooted around and pulled out a big brown envelope.

"Here's what I need," Kandy told us, and with that she unclasped the flap and brought out copies of some photos she'd found in that kitchen wall.

She handed them around. We got four sheets each, and there were three or four snapshots per page. Some of them were polaroids and others looked like wavy-edged Instamatic shots. Black and whites and color both. People in most of them, animals in a few.

"Look them over," Kandy said. "Take a day. Tell me if you see anybody you know. I'll come back in here tomorrow. First round's mine."

Then Kandy stalked straight out of The Anvil while we studied the sheets she'd left. The copies weren't all that sharp. There were people in front of a church we recognized and a man on a throne they still had in a corner of the Grange Hall. His hat was resting on his lap, and he appeared to have one eye. There were women who looked familiar to us along with assorted children. One of them, a girl, was on the back of a brindled dog.

We suspected them all for giblet donors, but we couldn't name anybody, not even the one-eyed man on the Grange Hall throne. That held anyway until Ken spoke up, and he didn't do that much. Ken had been some kind of engineer, had moved away and then come back.

He never prattled and rarely talked at all without invitation, so for him to be the one to start in was already unexpected even before he tapped on the snapshot of a lone child in a pasture. The kid was wearing some kind of striped sailor's shirt and could have made use of a comb.

"That boy there," Ken told us, "that'd be me."

2

We decided Kandy had a girlfriend before it turned out to be her sister. She'd brought over an actual suitcase full of stuff that Kandy required, and she spent a night with Kandy in Kandy's Laurel Lodge room. Then Kandy took her to Cuddy's for breakfast where we all got a daylight look.

If she'd turned out to be a girlfriend, it would have been an unexpected match since Kandy's sister (her name was Carol) looked entirely regular. She had ordinary hair and wore a cardigan and the kind of jeans that rode too high along with flats that ladies who garden and carry clutch purses usually wear. She and Kandy had a lively conversation about one of Carol's children who'd discovered cigarettes along with his daddy's vodka and was lately giving Carol loads of lip.

Kandy let Rick from Galveston go on with his work after six idle days, though she still kept everybody out of the kitchen and clear of that hole in the wall. The way we heard it, she'd visit Eaglesworth at odd hours unannounced. Rick would hear something when he thought his house was empty and go down to the kitchen where sometimes he'd find Kandy back among the studs and timbers turning her flashlight on and off.

Apparently, Rick went pissy the first time or two it happened. He had a few things to say about his rights and privileges and wondered what Kandy's bosses in Richmond would think of the job she was doing. Kandy would simply let him carry on.

She was not, as a rule, distractible. That's how it goes sometimes with misfits because the usual threats and insults don't hold any valence for them. Kandy's bosses didn't care where she was except well clear of Richmond. They were counting on her being somebody else's problem for a while, while Kandy personally wasn't the sort you could reach by yelling at her.

Kandy was aware, however, that she couldn't get away with telling us nothing. We prided ourselves on being decent, God-fearing folk. We certainly weren't giblet collectors or given to harboring that ilk, so we stayed anxious for Kandy to keep us up to speed on her inquiry, which Kandy seemed to appreciate and know.

But when she gave us news, Kandy only dribbled it out. Sometimes she'd do it by talking to the couple who ran our paper, or who ran the website anyway because the paper itself had died. All we had left of it were battered news boxes chained to various light poles around town.

The website was a part-time thing and looked it, and it only got updated about every week or three except during high-school football season when our beloved Golden Raiders (who ran the single wing because their coach was a mule-headed fool) would pile up losses that we liked to agonize about. The site would cover town council meetings, cats on offer from the pound, the weather, and there was usually a listing for somebody selling firewood — a full cord of seasoned oak on the page, which it never was in the truck.

The couple who ran it also worked at the shoe store the husband's family owned, and they snagged an interview with Kandy when she dropped in to buy some sneakers. Kandy had become aware of our walking path that ringed the abandoned gravel quarry, and everybody who went to see our GP usually ended up on it for a while. Early in the morning and evenings after work, you'd find a couple of dozen people out there strolling counterclockwise where three circuits was a mile.

It was Janet, the wife, who fitted her. She knew, of course, who Kandy was, and she took occasion to tell Kandy all about their website before daring to wonder if she could get a quote on the case as it stood. Janet had Kandy's foot in the Brannock device by then, which maybe gave her a touch of leverage, enough anyway to rate a statement.

"We're testing the candle box contents," Kandy said, "and pursuing some interesting leads."

So there was proof that Kandy, known to be capable of saying nothing, was pretty damn fine at saying next to nothing too.

She came back to The Anvil like she'd promised and bought us all a round before Ken could show her the snapshot of that child out in a pasture, a boy in need of a comb and a nose rag, and inform Kandy, "Me."

When he first told us, we'd asked Ken if he had any missing toes. We were convinced back then the photo people had been the source of the giblets and Ken could break the case open by naming the scoundrel who'd snipped him when he was a boy.

"Got everything," Ken told us, and he volunteered the same to Kandy.

"Remember who took this?" she asked Ken and pulled from her bag the actual snapshot. It had the ziggurat on the bottom like you'd get from a Land camera, the kind that opened up with bellows, and you'd take a shot and yank it clear. The photo was stamped with a date on the back, the year anyway — 1963.

Kandy let Ken handle it once she'd given him a lilac glove, and Ken sure took his time deciding if he recalled anything about it. He finally told us, "Used to love that shirt."

"How old were you?" Kandy asked him.

"Eight or nine, I guess."

"Where were you living?"

"Out on Pruitt." Ken pointed at nothing much and left us to tell Kandy Pruitt was a two-lane road in the county that ran by nothing mostly and went nowhere much.

"Was this taken there?" she asked Ken.

He made a Ken noise and squinted like maybe he wanted to drop a cueball himself.

That's about how it went no matter what Kandy asked, and we were generally sorry that the only pertinent witness we could offer up was Ken. He's just not a talker and never seems quite sure of what he thinks. Credit to Kandy, though, because she refused to be impatient with him.

"I think that's where Grandpa kept his cows."

"Uh huh. Ok," she told him. "Grandpa have a camera?" And she kept going around like that.

The rest of us tried to help her, but we weren't as calm and strategic as Kandy. That meant we chiefly told Ken that we'd sure remember if some of toe-snipping son-a-bitch had taken a picture of us.

"Who even had a camera like that?" a few of us decided to ask without even knowing exactly what a camera like that would look like until Kandy pulled up a photo of one and showed it to us on her phone. She left especially Ken the leisure to look at it for as long as he wanted while she nursed her Corona and entertained questions from the rest of us around.

We asked her about the kitchen niche and the state of the various giblets and wondered if she'd dug up anything, especially about the Crawley-Lowells because the talk around for years had been those two were nuts. Kandy sort of answered back, made us feel anyway like we were getting responses, but once we'd taken time to consider and turn over what she'd said, we realized we'd not ended up with much.

Eventually, we directed her to the historical society ladies.

"Ask Joyce and them." It was Edgar who told her. The rest of us nodded and groaned.

Those historical society ladies were comprehensively well informed, but they had no editorial sense among them. You could approach them wanting to know one thing and just one thing alone and still find yourself under an avalanche of indiscriminate piffle.

Since we couldn't move the ball for Kandy, Joyce and them were her next best chance. We all knew it, but we all regretted it for her and warned her they were chatty. By then Kandy had probably decided anybody would be better than us, a bunch of half-lit geezers in a dingy saloon.

When she left us, Kandy stopped off to talk to a guy sitting at the bar. We were aware of him a little. He did cut-rate home repairs for people who didn't want a permit or necessarily needed precision. He was the sort willing to go in your crawlspace to sister up your rotting joists, would slather sealant on your chimney flashing until the rain stopped coming in, and would fix your crumbling brickwork by shooting Sakrete out of a tube. Nothing had collapsed on anybody yet that they could hold him for, so he was at liberty to come nights to The Anvil and talk to Randi's cleavage, watch sports on her three TVs, and eat her complimentary party mix.

Kandy chatted him up like she knew him, leaned against the bar right beside the man and explained a thing his way. He listened. He nodded. He left half a beer and came off of his stool. He followed Kandy out the door, which we got floored about.

"Did he just go off with her?"

A couple of us said it out loud, and the rest of us wondered what sort of planet we were occupying where a professional woman like Kandy would proposition a stranger at a bar in a town where she didn't live and take him back to her motel room for a wrangle.

Some of us had children about Kandy's age who we'd assumed were cautious and upstanding, but maybe they'd go off with a jackleg carpenter they'd never clapped eyes on before.

We knew there were women around with a taste for roughnecks, and not just the ones in tube tops who looked in daylight like they'd knife you, but we'd thought Kandy was some other kind of girl.

We were deep into toxic and unsavory assessments of her by the time that boy came back in and plopped down on his stool. He didn't look especially serviced and satisfied, didn't look any different at all and had only been out of The Anvil for maybe fifteen minutes. Because we're not unreasonable people, we put Kandy the slattern on hold and sent Paul over to interrogate the fellow.

"What was that all about?" Paul asked him as he jabbed a thumb towards the door.

That boy watched a foul tip, took a swig from his warm beer. "Jumped her car," he said.

~~~~~~

Rick from Galveston's girlfriend came up, and we got the feeling she didn't tell him about it until she was in Tennessee because we saw Rick scrambling around after groceries and bed sheets and shower rod rings. He had no time to chew the fat. "Company" is what he called her, and he was clearly excited but in an I-think-I'm-having-a-seizure way.

She couldn't find the house and stopped at the Citgo, asked Teddy for directions and described the place by telling him that it was big and old. She didn't even know the proper name but had a picture on her phone.

"Just keep going," Teddy told her.

She didn't thank him or anything but went back to her car, a flashy German coupe, and let her dog out to pee on the pump island. His name was Carlton, and she'd tell you loudly he had cataracts as a way of explaining why Carlton was given to running into things. He also had bangs down over his eyes, which couldn't have been much help.

She called herself Angela. Rick only ever called her Angie and never introduced her as his girlfriend or anything really. She was always just Angie, the female beside him he felt like he ought to name. She made it clear to us she didn't approve of a thing Rick had gotten up to from the moment he'd driven out of Galveston.

Angie lived in a waterfront condo, or "good as" was how she'd put it, where she didn't need to do a thing but run the sweeper on the rugs. She couldn't begin to understand the urge to renovate, especially a massive hulk of a house like Rick had taken on with Eaglesworth.

We didn't like her, of course. We don't like most people, but we put some thought and energy into not liking her. We didn't care for her terrier either who needed a hair ribbon and a couple of swats. We capped it off by not approving at all of her German coupe, which was so low-slung it scraped every time she turned off of the street.

To give her some credit, though, Rick's girl did serve as a bracing dose of near steady irritation. Rick got most of it, but she saved some for the rest of us as well. She'd just been with us a couple of days when she had a fit at the meat counter in Dooley's where she'd damn well expected to find some chicken that wasn't a wing or a back.

They had a butcher call button in Dooley's, but we all knew it wasn't connected, and Rick's girl messed with it to no effect for long enough to steam her. Given that she kind of stayed steam, that didn't take much time at all. There was nobody official to yell at beyond the boy who restocks soup. He suffers from what his mother likes to call emotional problems, but it's a trifle more severe than that, which is why he just restocks soup.

Angie barked at him until he'd scurried off to fetch Dooley's little sister who showed up to administer a jolt of customer service.

"What are you carrying on about?" Dooly's sister wanted to know.

Angie ended up getting expelled from Dooley's before she'd reached peak indignation. She finally achieved that in the parking lot and stood there yelling at the storefront for a while.

Glenn sent Deputy Doby over because it came through sounding like a fight. He rolled in with his beacon lit and started out calling Angie "sugar", which earned Doby the brand of scalding response he wasn't used to from girls. Then she slipped into her German coupe and exited the lot in such a hurry that she left her tailpipe and her muffler and her catalytic converter behind.

Rick eventually came to collect them and made a kind of apology tour that started in Dooley's and ended up with Sheriff Glenn down at the station. Deputy Rachel was her own brand of hothead, so Glenn was sympathetic because he'd done more than a little apologizing himself.

"People know it's not you," Glenn told Rick.

But that wasn't quite the case since what people actually knew is that life is full of choices, and we all have to answer at least a little for the ones we make. So the longer Rick's lady friend stayed around, the more we learned about them both.

Angie was scary and worked part-time back in Texas as a legal aid. She had a way of delivering threats that sounded darkly judicial, and she did it mostly from behind the wheel of her coupe. She was a terror on the roads. She zipped through town, turned where she shouldn't, parked where nobody ever had, and if you impeded her in any way (like by crossing a street or something) she'd threaten to go all "true bill on your ass".

We didn't know what that meant, but it sure sounded unpleasant. Rick couldn't explain it either, though he'd apologize nonetheless. He did a load of that in the two weeks Angie stayed, and she probably wouldn't have left when she did but for Carlton's conjunctivitis that Angie decided he'd picked up from rabbits in the yard at Eaglesworth. Our vet tried to straighten her out on that but just got shouted down.

She was our new vet, fresh from Blacksburg, and she did everything with blood work. She couldn't look at an animal to save her life and tell you what it had. Our old vet used to do that. He might have been wrong about half the time, but he was never anything short of confident. He'd explain how to make some potion at home with vinegar and linseed oil, something guaranteed to stink enough to convince you you were helping. The new girl drew blood and then sold you pricey pharmaceuticals but in doses way too small to do much good.

She liked to tell us she was cautious. Useless was the better word.

Consequently, we weren't entirely unhappy that Angie found occasion to snarl at our new veterinarian. That girl needed far more of that sort of thing than she was likely to get from us. But there was no convincing Angie that rabbits weren't infecting Carlton, so either Rick from Galveston had to kill them all or Angie was going home. In this instance, Rick could have his way by doing next to nothing. He cleaned his rifle for a day, and then Angie packed and left.

It's hard enough to live with wholesale construction, but there was also a police investigation largely in the person of Kandy who'd show up unannounced for basement time and stand in that wall hollow fooling with her flashlight. Angie tried to boss her, attempted to set some ground rules, might even have ranted at Kandy and true billed her a time or two, but Kandy was accomplished at not much caring what other folks thought or wanted. She had stuff on her mind and a job to do.

So Angie arrived mad and left madder, and a boy we know who was up there shifting Rick's septic tank around, happened to be on hand when she climbed in her coupe and departed.

"She's kind of a pistol," that septic tank boy told Rick, and Rick apologized.

Soon after, we started seeing more of Rick around town. He'd eat supper at Cuddy's and stop by The Anvil, even rolled a few games every now and then over at Atomic, and he often came down for the farmer's market in the Unitarian lot.

He didn't talk much, except maybe to Randi whose job was to get yammered at, and a few of us made an effort to try to loosen Rick up. We shared with him various tales we knew of the historic goings on up at Eaglesworth, and they were frequently wild and lively without us having to stretch them too much.   Particularly where it came to the Avent with the turpentine fortune because he'd kept a rigorous journal that a professor in Maryland had found.

It had turned up in a box of books he'd bought blind at an auction in Hagerstown, and he'd taken particular interest in it largely because of the sketches. The professor's field was botany, and that Avent had drawn scores of flowers, which were frequently in the vicinity of much less seemly, lurid stuff. That Avent, it turned out, had been an avid student of female anatomy, and he didn't just roll around drunk on sherry at his gentlemen's soirees but put pen to paper and made detailed studies of his guests in the throes of business probably best left unsketched.

It took the professor a year or two to see past all the flowers and realize that journal might well be more notable for the sexy stuff. He got an edition put out for the general horny reader, and Rick from Galveston allowed he'd never so much as heard of the thing.

In fact, Rick was appallingly ignorant of Eaglesworth's history, so we made a point of inflicting some on him every chance we got. We didn't want him to abandon his work on the place, no matter how tempted he might feel. Rick had drainage problems, a family of flying squirrels in his attic, and termites had eaten about halfway through one of his chestnut sills. That meant a corner needed to get jacked up, and Rick was worrying about brickwork failing. So we were keen to keep him tuned in to Eaglesworth's pedigree.

Rick tolerated us well enough up to a point, but with his lady friend back in Texas, he soon got interested in Randi, and the two of them had one of Randi's usual sorts of flings. That girl has her pick of patrons because she's freckled and seems sympathetic and never altogether buttons her shirt.

The trouble is Randi, at bottom, isn't interested in men. She never takes one up intending him for a keeper because fresh candidates wander in and out of The Anvil all the time. Not always completely fresh — we are a backwater after all — but guys who've not been in for a while because maybe they took a wife roll in again and get reminded of Randi and her shirt.

We don't think of her as slutty because Randi's too forthright for that. She tolerates men, just not in a lasting way, and that's where things get thorny.

Rick from Galveston was no different from most of the rest of us guys. He could get himself worked up and anxious over the girls he couldn't have, or couldn't have anyway beyond the two or three nights that Randi routinely allowed, and then you'd show back up at The Anvil and she'd have moved down a stool or two.

Randi was always clear about who she was and blunt about what she wanted, but men have a way of over prizing their pull.

So Rick went through the standard-issue romance ringer with Randi. She laughed at his quips and took him home where she explained what she was about and how anything they might get up to did not constitute a commitment. Rick said he understood, the way men will, and then they rolled around.

After a few days, Randi moved on. She always does. Not even necessarily to another Anvil patron since Randi is perfectly capable of dropping a guy and going fallow. That's the galling thing. She can prefer even nothing to you.

We'd tried to warn Rick, but that never really works what with the freckles and the half-buttoned shirt, so soon enough he was heartsick and not worth talking to because if he came into The Anvil he'd just sit at the bar and moon. Consequently, we turned our attention to Kandy and went digging and snooping around to see if we could put our time to good purpose by finding out exactly who she was.

It turned out Kandy had been an equestrian once, concentrating on dressage. Her people came from up by Winchester where they lived on a sprawling farm that had passed to Kandy's family from her mother's father. He'd been a pulpwood timber baron, had clear-cut huge swathes of the Alleghenies, the parts he didn't live near and wouldn't have to see. His farmhouse was a federalist four-on-on. We'd dug up pictures of it, and it had droopy white oaks around it and was in prime nick for its age.

Kandy went to school at Sweet Briar. Given the horsiness, that wasn't surprising, but it sure didn't fit the lumbering, tattooed, ear-metal Kandy we knew. After she graduated, Kandy caught on at the prosecutor's office in Charlottesville and then shifted over to Richmond and started working for the state police. They mostly fool with stuff the counties can't afford to handle, lack the wattage and manpower to pull off. As best we could determine, Kandy had chiefly worked white-collar crime and seemed to have some kind of math background from college.

If Kandy had ever headed a case remotely like our candle box full of toes, we couldn't find evidence of it anywhere online. The closest she'd come was an embezzlement thing where the executive they'd fingered tried to end it all. At the last moment, he lost his nerve and fired a round through a window washer. But that was an odd one for Kandy. Her chief lot was harmless schemers and dodgy math.

We were a bit surprised to discover that Kandy had been engaged to marry. Her intended was named Douglas, and he was a tree trimmer from Wheeling. Not the kind who shimmies up trunks but the sort who owns a fleet of trucks. We'd found the wedding announcement in The Winchester Star but then turned up a squib from a few months later about the engagement being called off due to "an unfortunate development".

We decided Kandy probably had second thoughts because she was picky and independent, and for good measure we gave Douglas a girlfriend in a trailer park. The Kandy who'd come to us sure didn't look like bride material. She didn't look, of course, like state police material either. So even after we'd poked around and dredged up all that stuff on Kandy, we still didn't feel terribly illuminated.

We were secretly hoping — though we never came out and said as much — that our candle box full of human toes and who exactly had packed and hid it would make for the sort of ghastly tale that folks would detour off the highway about. That way we'd stop being just the picturesque town that used to have a timber bandstand, the place Longstreet's army had rushed past in retreat.

Better still, those giblets were old and dried up and so were historical as well, and in truth it didn't really matter if we ever found out who'd nipped them since the mystery of never knowing might be kind of a grabber too.

We had boxed up bits hidden back in the wall of a massive old house on a hilltop and an odd sort of woman detective come clear from Richmond to sort our stuff out. So there was drama already kicking off even before the fire. It wasn't a grand, destructive blaze. Eaglesworth was far too soggy for that. Years of busted windows had let the damp seep into the plaster, so there was only so much harm a shorted out vermin box could do.

3

Kandy paid a call on the historical society ladies in their special room in the library basement. They've long called it a gallery, but it isn't open to the public, and they claim to give tours upon request but can never seem to find the time. So they buy items of interest to them with historical society donations and then keep them mostly locked away for themselves.

They're not trained authorities but just a trio of hobbyists who have access to all the most pertinent books because they're also in charge of the library upstairs. For the rest of us that means a half dozen volumes on colonial crockery and a fat biography or three of George Mason's second wife but hardly any installments in the series about the alcoholic detective in Milwaukee who carries a sap and a condom and makes liberal use of both.

We felt like we knew what those ladies would say to Kandy when she visited, and we had a fair idea of what she'd probably tell them back. They couldn't be direct about anything and usually started in with the Pilgrims. If you went to them keen to find out when your people got an indoor toilet, you'd have to hear about the Jamestown settlement first.

The way we imagined it, Kandy would get ushered into the gallery in the basement and would show those women the candle box she would almost surely have brought along. That would prompt those girls to visit on Kandy a general history of candle boxes, particularly the ones that had arrived in the Chesapeake Bay on the Susan Constant or the Godspeed.

Joyce was the only one of the historical society ladies a regular human could talk to, and our guy for that was Edgar who'd taken her out on several dates. They saw a movie. They went to a buffet. They heard a string quartet in Culpeper. And then Edgar tried to carry Joyce to a ball game out towards Richmond, but she changed her mind before they could get there and asked Edgar to take her home.

Apparently, Edgar was wearing fan gear — the hat, the jersey, the stretchy pants — and Joyce decided that was more of a cultural deficit than she could fix or stand.

Joyce would still exchange pleasantries with Edgar. She seemed to feel sorry for him like you would for a dog you'd dropped off at the pound. Joyce had since found herself a more suitable man, a lanky insurance adjuster, who always looked miserable enough to make Edgar happy she'd moved on.

So once we knew Kandy had visited those women in their basement gallery, we sent Edgar to pump Joyce for anything about that meeting she might say. He was rewarded with "That girl's different" and news that curly maple was also known as fiddle back and tiger stripe sometimes too.

We already knew Kandy was different, and we didn't care about curly maple, which was the basic problem with our trio of historical society ladies. They belabored the stuff you had a grip on already and buried you in details you had no appetite to know.

Then Eaglesworth caught fire, and while tidying up after the smoke and the light charring, Rick's plaster man found some damn thing else in a pantry wall. Three damn things really. A shoe, a keyhole saw, and another snapshot. Rick wanted him not to say anything, especially to Kandy from Richmond, and the plaster man was quick to allow he'd found stuff in walls before.

The shoe and the saw wouldn't have been a problem to keep under wraps, but the snapshot drew him up short. It was attached to a timber crossbeam, was skewered on a four-penny nail, and he recognized the girl in the photo. Everybody did except for Rick.

"Nellie," the plaster guy told him. "She was an odd bird all right."

So Kandy got summoned in the end and went up for a look. She had Rick's boys dismantle the pantry, but they just found an old rat's nest and some half-chewed, corroded wiring.

Kandy studied the photo of Nellie and asked the plaster guy, "Odd how?"

Nellie had known four distinct stages in her life. There was the childhood cruelty and casual carnage of Nellie the roughneck girl. She'd hurt pets — cats primarily but a lapdog once as well — and had injured playmates, often with rocks she'd throw at point-blank range.

Nellie had grown into a graceful and comely young woman with a taste for rough, half-tamed men. She preferred the sort who would knock her around, and then she'd answer back even harder. Twice she'd done the brand of harm to men they'd needed surgeons to fix. They'd forgive her as a rule and be just slightly more tame ever after.

She finally married a guy, a meek one, and kicked him around along with her kids. She didn't seem to need liquor or drugs or anything beyond meanness to do it. Nellie eventually got locked up for tossing her son out of a tree. He broke his wrist when he landed on his sister.

She spent a year in regular jail and twice that long at the state nuthouse over by Staunton. She came out calm-ish and a lot less dainty than she'd gone in. She was thick and pale and hollow-eyed, and she lived out in the country in a tenant house by a feedlot for a while. She took long walks on the roadsides and, if luck smiled upon her, she'd find cow flop to throw at passing cars.

Then Nellie disappeared. Nobody saw her at all for a month or three. No walks. No cow-flop flinging. She didn't show herself in town. She failed to pay her power bill, and they sent a man to disconnect her. He knocked on her door to give her one last chance before he pulled her service. The door wasn't latched and swung wide open. That let the stink of Nellie gone to her sweet Savior come boiling out.

The cops eventually found her in a closet, just sitting in there greasy and dead. She was wearing a bathrobe and a pair of rubber mucking boots. That closet door wasn't latched or anything. She could have come out if she'd wanted. Aside from being dead and smelly, she wasn't damaged at all.

The sheriff at the time was the one before Glenn, and he was probably even slightly more worthless. He invited citizens to come forward with any information they might have on Nellie, and a fellow from out in the county we only ever knew as Mickey did come in to the PD one day and got a meeting with the sheriff to acquaint him with what some of Nellie's cow manure had done to the finish on his Dodge.

Mickey's statement was in the file that Kandy turned up along with the county doctor's report, which failed to identify a cause of death but did make passing mention that Nellie was missing a toe. The doc hadn't bothered to say which one, if she'd been born without it or if somebody had lopped it off, and that was enough for Kandy to approach Glenn about an exhumation since she had precious little going for her otherwise.

Glenn was against it, of course, because Glenn likes to stand in opposition to all forms of community upset. Glenn advocates smooth sailing in local human affairs, no matter what you have to ignore to get it. Yes, he will arrest civilians and make judicial trouble for them but always only eventually and after a great while. Glenn wasn't about to see the sense in digging Nellie up after close to twenty years in the ground.

"Say her toe's in that box," Glenn told Kandy, "where does that get you?"

It was a fair question, and Kandy told Glenn back, "Better to know than not."

She had the pull and the budget and didn't actually need Glenn, so he could tell her, "I wouldn't," and retire into the background. Nathan drew up the papers they required, but then it became apparent that nobody anywhere knew where Nellie was.

When a ranty old woman who throws cow flop gets found dead in her closet, especially one who's long since shed her people and has spent a while in Western State, folks aren't likely to be too particular about where exactly they put her. It was a wonder really they hadn't just popped her right into the furnace.

She proved to be at the memorial park out past the middle school. The place was a farm and then a failed shopping plaza before it got repurposed as a sprawling pasture for human remains. There's a statue of Jesus on the road in and a traffic circle around him, some cut-rate mausoleums in back where the marble is all busted up.

Kandy got ahold of the company that owns and operates our memorial park. They had a central office up in Pennsylvania and two dozen similar people pastures scattered across these United States.

One of their reps kept making confident promises to Kandy that he would soon send her a map of our memorial park with all the residents identified and plotted, but that string of promises was all she ever got. Kandy gave up and did the smart thing. She raised a kind of local posse by tacking notices up to the various cork boards around and requesting civilian assistance on the Eaglesworth giblet case. We were nosy and eager, and it didn't hurt that Kandy promised refreshments and a light lunch as well.

So we showed up out at the memorial park on a Saturday morning in our long sleeves and our hats against the sun because while that place had a half dozen cedars of Lebanon where you turned in off the road, the tallest thing out on the burial ground was usually a pot full of plastic lilies. The headstones were all just blocks of granite not quite the size of a shoe box, and they were engraved with names and dates, an American flag for veterans. There wasn't room for shout-outs to Jesus or trumpeting angels and lambs and such.

We were looking for Nellie Marie Boykins, possibly Nellie Marie Pascal since Kandy couldn't know if they'd packed her away under her own or her married name. She had kind of Nellie's death date, the year anyway — 1997 — and Kandy gave us each a patch of ground to cover. She said her colleague would roll in noon-ish with what she called a "splendid" lunch.

There were fourteen of us, and the fact that we needed most of a day speaks to the sprawl of that memorial park and all of our friends and neighbors in it. The whole exercise served as a grim reminder of who exactly had gone away. We walked down our rows and checked our headstones and here and there ran across people we hadn't even realized were dead. Maybe never knew it. More likely forgot it. That's how it is out in the countryside with folks you only saw once or twice a year.

We found Nellie late. Our splendid lunch had already come and gone. Nathan had brought it out from the catering lady. A bag of chips, a chunk of apple, and half a ham salad sandwich along with a sweet dill pickle, two if you were lucky, and we got canned sodas from Dooley's. The brand nobody's ever heard of with the dents and the dusty tops.

Nellie was out just beyond a trio of Hazlips who'd been killed in a car crash together when their boy, who carried snakes around, let one of them get loose. North of Nellie was one of the Samson boys who wouldn't have cared for her company. People still sometimes wonder how, when he had his coronary, he managed to pile up on the sidewalk in spite of the massive stick up his ass.

There was a Crater south of Nellie who'd stood on the wrong side of a sawed tree, and the woman to Nellie's east was a Comstock from South Carolina who used to sell corn and melons and tomatoes out of the back of her Country Squire wagon. She was memorable because she swore like eight sailors if you'd roped them together and lit them on fire.

So it was several hours of baking sun, fear of death, and nostalgia, but we ended up with Nellie, and then the backhoe guy rolled in. Kandy was using an Emerson brother, the one who never spoke. He mostly dug trenches for sewer and water lines, and you sure could tell it by the way he brought Nellie's coffin up. Let's call it insensitive, more vertical than not.

It seemed there for a couple of minutes that Nellie might just spill out on the ground, and that would have been quite a detail to add to our giblet story, so we didn't care how ferociously Kandy encouraged us to leave. Our crew stayed in that memorial park and gawked.

That Emerson finally got Nellie up onto his flatbed truck and then drove her out towards the interstate to the clinic. They had a solitary doctor at that place and a slew of not-quite doctors. They charged flat fees, kept box-store hours, and Kandy had worked a deal to get one of them to have a look at Nellie. Take a tissue sample for analysis. See about that missing toe.

Nellie got unboxed in the basement around back. We didn't, of course, get to see it, but the ex-sister-in-law of a fellow we know helped draw the screws out of the casket lid. She told us Nellie was in far better condition than they'd feared. Shriveled and shrunk up, naturally, but not terribly rotted and awful, and it proved easy to check her out because she was only wearing a shirt. A nice shirt with pearl buttons and ruffles on the front but no other scrap of clothing at all.

Kandy (the way we heard it) kept crowding in for a look, and the actual doctor himself finally came down and helped with the tissue sample while Kandy hovered with her phone and took a bunch of snaps. Nellie was missing the little toe on her left foot, and they could tell it hadn't been nipped any time around her death because it was completely scarred over. The doc guessed it could well have come off when Nellie was a child.

Then they fitted her lid back on and strapped her down on the truck again. By the time that Emerson drove her out and put her right back where we'd found her, our crew had reconvened in The Anvil to float our theories and air our suspicions over Randi's wretched popcorn shrimp and passable chicken wings.

We'd been zeroing in on suspects. We had three we liked in particular. They'd all been collectors and fairly showy about it. Two of them were still alive but off in nursing homes or somewhere while the third one was five or six years in the ground. He was the creepiest one of the lot and was conveniently from Idaho. We preferred thinking whoever had assembled those giblets in that curly maple box had to be from somewhere else entirely. We could make our peace with being hayseed underachievers but we hated to cross the line to bloodthirsty psychosis.

Better still, the Idaho guy had come to us well into his thirties, so he'd arrived shaped and tainted and already peculiar. He did marry a local girl, one of the Simpsons, but she threw him over for better stock in time. He was some kind of scientist, held one of those government jobs that kept him from telling anybody what he did.

As a hobby, he collected bugs at first but soon graduated to small rodents, mostly voles and mice, woods rats and squirrels. He'd gas them and skin them and soak them in buckets full of chemicals that would strip the meat away and bleach the bones. Then he'd firm up the skeletons with epoxy and put them in the sorts of jars where a sane man would stick a boat.

The guy was known locally for being standoffish and odd, and his ex-wife told about him wandering through their house at night. He'd talk to himself and drink Old Grandad mixed with (for Godsakes) milk. So he was a little off and unfriendly and from way out west, and if he needed to dissolve you in a tub he absolutely could.

While we had three possible suspects, we all liked our Idaho nut best, and over shrimp and wings we decided to hand him off to Kandy. She had a tip line that Nathan managed, but we figured that was all cranks and fools, and we were determined to tell Kandy what we thought face to face.

We should have used our wait time to come up with that gentleman's full name and try maybe to locate one of his skeletons in a bottle. He'd sell them at the flea market, so there were bound to be a few around, but we didn't get to any of that, and Kandy rolled into The Anvil before we were armed with terribly much.

Two of our crew approached her at the bar. Roland was one of them. We like to send him to talk to people because Roland's got a chatty knack. He's perfectly comfortable going on for a quarter hour about nothing, and while he waited for Randi to freshen up his Jack and ginger, Roland had kind of a back and forth with Kandy.

"See the history ladies?" he asked her by way of preamble and palaver.

"Heard a hell of a lot about Jamestown," Kandy told him back.

~~~~~

The truth is we approved of Kandy in about every way a crew of men can approve of a girl. She seemed to have no patience at all for the stuff we had no patience for, and she hardly ever went out of her way to be cordial or polite. Kandy wasn't rude, just big and quiet sometimes, and she rarely seemed to feel the need to ladle on much froth.

We liked that about her, and she had no use for Glenn or the associate pastor who went around town saying Christian things to people. You'd be counting your change or trying to remember what you'd left home to get when he'd sidle up and tell you, "All things work together for good to them that love God." Then he'd grip you by the shoulder and wink like he'd made a car payment for you.

Once Roland finally got around to filling her in on our Idaho bone bleacher, Kandy pulled out the pad she carried, a little dime-store spiral thing, and jotted down 'Idaho' and jotted down 'squirrels', jotted down 'Simpson' too. She'd never come right out and tell us to leave her alone or advise us to cork up our speculation, but Kandy would sometimes make a throaty noise we'd take for instructive, and she'd go back to her beer or her cutlet or continue towards her filthy car, and we'd wait for the next chance to catch her fresh and tell her something else.

Idaho guy's ex-wife was a widow and lived in the next town over. Kandy drove out to see her because Kandy was thorough that way, and she took tea with the woman since she ran a tea shop in a spot where no tea shop was demanded or required. They could have used an orthodontist or maybe a shoe repair guy but they got Darjeeling and dulcimer music and lemon squares instead.

The way we heard it, that Simpson woman barely remembered the Idaho guy. She'd been young when they married, and she'd had her regrets a day or two after the wedding. His name was Gary, as it turned out, and his ex didn't paint him as especially peculiar.

"Just a man," she told Kandy. "You know how they are."

Gary had been some sort of chemist, and Kandy told his ex she'd heard about the tree squirrels and the voles.

"That was after me," the woman said. "I wouldn't have stood for that."

"So he was . . . normal with you?" Kandy asked her, or something very much like it, and that Simpson woman circled back to, "You know how they are."

We were getting a lesson in police work. There was no urgency to it, given the vintage of our case, so we got to see how this sort of business could be a monumental trudge. Kandy drove places and talked to people. She and Nathan (we had to think) debated possibilities, accumulated evidence — or something sort of like it — and tried as best they were able to make a story out of the thing.

But there was little to tell, just a box full of giblets, a dead woman missing a toe, and an Idaho bone bleacher whose ex-wife insisted he was no worse or better than any other man she'd known. Then the reports started coming in, thankfully, from the state police lab in Richmond where they established that one of the toes in the box had definitely come off Nellie, though they had no way of knowing how or when.

So even if our candle box case wasn't quite a full-blown story, we were certainly getting better details to make up stuff about. The business was definitely Nellie related, so Kandy was already moving the ball before Professor Reginald Duff arrived on the scene and stopped in at Eaglesworth to have a look around.

Rick found him wandering through the house. He'd had free reign of the place for probably the best part of an hour because everybody thought he was working up a price for some kind of job. Two of the chimney stacks had to be relined, and there was a fellow due to give Rick a quote for varnishing the floors. So Reginald Duff in the house wouldn't have seemed strange at all except for his yellow flip-flops and his three-piece tweed suit.

He was a big, hairy bloke. We all got a look at the man in time, but there at first it was only Rick and one of the plumber's helpers who caught sight of him strolling around.

"Help you?" Rick asked.

Reginald Duff raised his hands like a preacher might. "The few assume to be the deputies," he said, "but they are often only the despoilers of the many."

He was a professor, a college philosophy instructor on that campus out in the valley that the Christian Scientists bought, and he had the volume and bearing of the sort of academic who'd gotten used to making pronouncements to batches students at a time.

Rick said, "All right," and pulled out his phone to call the law.

Deputy Jason rolled up. That would be large Deputy Jason and not the Jason who primarily works the desk and has a blood disorder. This was husky scholarship lacrosse Deputy Jason who looked sensational in even his baggy county uniform. Unfortunately, this Deputy Jason was also aggressively not bright, was one of those not bright people who insists on being loud about it.

Jason immediately got into an argument with Professor Reginald Duff. It mostly hinged on the professor pairing flip flops with a suit, and not just any suit but a busy tweed with tiny checks and speckles and more tabs and buttons on the jacket and vest than you'll ever see off the rack.

Deputy Jason had a long look at Reginald Duff's ensemble before asking the man, "What's up with you, buddy?"

Reginald Duff informed Deputy Jason, "Change alone is eternal, perpetual, immortal."

Deputy Jason snorted and cut loose with four syllable's worth of, "What?"

We know now that was Schopenhauer, and the professor added beyond it, "The world is my idea," which proved to be Schopenhauer too.

Nobody thought to tell Kandy about him for pretty much half a day, and the professor sat in a holding cell in a paper jumpsuit. Or rather he stood in a holding cell anyway and talked to the mortar joints while Deputy Rachel went through his pockets and found two Canadian quarters, a half a roll of mints, a stubby golf pencil, and scraps of paper that somebody (him, they guessed) had drawn child-like sketches on. A tree with a cloud in the sky and the sun. A duck from about the neck up. A stick man with what looked like a broadsword. A house with flowers in the yard. Some kind of squiggly design that kind of resembled a spearhead.

Rachel couldn't find a wallet or a license or a charge card, but she did eventually come across a man's name, Morris Neville-Jones. It was stamped inside the tweed trousers on one of the waistband tags.

She popped into the holding cell long enough to try that name on the professor. He seemed happy for the company and told Rachel back, "What Paul says about Peter tells us more about Paul than about Peter."

Deputy Rachel is ordinarily a woman of scant patience. She's even worse on her bloat days, and she was having one of those, so it was fine with her if Morris Neville-Jones just stood around for a while.

Kandy happened to see the tweed suit because Rachel had left it piled next to the big box of creamer packets, and Kandy couldn't help but pay attention to it due to how it was loud and wooly and stank. Deputy Jason, who was still doing paperwork on the professor, pointed at the suit and told Kandy where he'd run across the owner of it and why.

Kandy talked to the professor through the peephole first because Deputy Jason had assured her the man was kind of a nut.

"They say you were over at Eaglesworth," was how Kandy started in.

The professor scratched and stretched. He found Kandy in the door slot and stepped her way as he told her, "Curiosity is the lust of the mind."

"See?" Deputy Jason said.

But Kandy was a Sweet Briar graduate who hadn't squandered her time on campus with the brand of foolishness most girls that age get up to. It probably helped her academically that she was large and lumpy and so failed to hang with the clique of coeds who weren't about to learn anything.

"Thomas Hobbes," Kandy said. That only rated a squint from Jason. "Curiosity is the lust of the mind."

Kandy didn't have a room in the annex for talking to people like the professor, nothing where a citizen could come in and she could hook him to a table, so Sheriff Glenn insisted she use their spot up in the regular office, which meant they'd all be standing behind the glass watching Kandy work. Most particularly Deputy Rachel who had few demands on her time, a leading perk of being the sheriff's girlfriend, and she craved proximity to any woman who was north of one fourteen.

"You drive here?" That was the very first question Kandy bothered to ask after dropping into the chair across the table from Reginald Duff.

He raised an open hand. "A wise man proportions his belief to the evidence," he said.

"Catch a ride?" Kandy asked him.

"Be a philosopher but, amid all your philosophy, be still a man."

Outside at the glass Glenn and Rachel and them were all floating what they'd have done by then, the brand of pressure they would have applied. Especially Deputy Doby who was a martial arts enthusiast, if that's what you call a man who watches videos on the web and occasionally tosses his nephew around in the yard. But even the rest of them were persuaded they would have smacked the professor already because they seemed to come at the job believing the public owes them the truth. As if the truth were a definite thing, like some citizen's lost billfold, that you could just pull out and hand over to the law.

Kandy didn't hold with any of that, and the professor most decidedly refused to. The truth was always partial and shifting, depending on where you were. Kandy had located in one of the pockets of Reginald Duff's suit coat a tag from a men's shop on George Street in Edinburgh. She showed it to the professor.

"Buy it over there?"

"All things excellent are as difficult as they are rare."

They'd figure out later (once they'd listened to everything back) that he was going from Hobbes to Hume to Locke to Spinoza to Descartes sometimes too. That was the ink the professor liked to spray. Eventually, Reginald Duff dropped his philosophers long enough to inform Kandy that the paper suit he was wearing was giving him a rash, so she let him have his tweed one back.

"Conquer yourself," he said as he pulled on his scratchy pants, "rather than the world."

It turned out that suit was from a Glasgow thrift shop where Morris Neville-Jones must have dumped it. The professor had bought the yellow flip-flops at a dime store up in Martinsburg. Kandy had noticed first thing that the professor was missing the right little toe from his filthy foot.

Kandy had the professor walk her through the drawings that had come out of his tweed suit pockets. The house with the tree. The man with the sword. The duck but just from the neck up. He wasn't interested in talking much about them, not directly anyway. He told Kandy, "Compassion is the basis of morality," and several other things.

It was different with the spearhead sketch. The professor drummed on that one with his finger and came out with a string of stuff that proved half Scripture, half brainiac chatter. Then he just sat there in silence for a couple of minutes, and Kandy was about to roll along to something else entirely when the professor told her, "Eaglesworth," just flat and ordinary like maybe he was sane.

"Have you been up there before today?" Kandy asked him.

He tapped on the spearhead again.

Kandy had photos to hand, some of them the snapshots from back in the walls and some just pictures she had taken inside the house and out on the grounds. She plucked out the best one available to her of Eaglesworth from down by the road and held it up for the professor to see.

"So you know this place?"

The professor took that photo from her for a careful, deliberate look. At the bottom of the picture, where the driveway met the road, was an old iron gate that had rusted on its hinges and was leaning against some scrub. Whoever had made it had spelled out Eaglesworth in sweeping letters across the top with scrollwork decorating either end.

That's what the professor pointed out to Kandy. A couple of rusty flowers that looked a bit like spearheads. Lilies of a sort is what they were, some kind of half-assed fleur-de-lis.

The professor hadn't captured them exactly on his dirty scrap of paper, but for a nut in a tweed suit and yellow flip-flops, he'd come pretty damn close.

He handed the snapshot back to Kandy. "What worries you, masters you," he said.

TWO

1

We wondered if our culprit hadn't maybe rented a room up at Eaglesworth during that stretch when the Lowell widow was taking tenants in. We couldn't recall exactly all the flotsam who'd lived up there, but there'd been a big, blonde carpet layer everybody knew around town because he drove a sky-blue GTO and was working a kind of grift.

He'd bring in his sample book and let you pick from high-quality stock, but then the carpet he'd lay was always something else entirely, cheap and smelly and shiny, but he'd insist you'd ordered it. The very best you could get was him taking it up, but by then you'd paid him half . He finally made the mistake of laying green shag for a woman out by Boyce. It ended up looking a lot like over ambitious astroturf, and her sons skipped the complaining and just beat the fellow up.

There was also a girl at Eaglesworth for probably close to a year. She wore a stretchy bandage on one leg and a floppy hat against the sun. One of our crew remembered her at the Bel-Air once or twice. It was a drive-in movie theater, and she used to show up there on foot and sit on the bench up front by the monkey bars. He worked there, our guy. His job was to wander around and pick up trash while frustrating fornication.

He remembered the girl drank apple brandy out of a pint bottle and smoked skinny White Owl cigars.

This was all in the wake of Professor Reginald Duff arriving in town. They got contentious about him over at the PD because Kandy wanted to keep him, but aside from simple trespass, Glenn had no cause to hold the man. If the professor had a fixed address, he couldn't remember what it was, and it appeared likely if they cut him loose, he'd stick out his thumb and get gone.

Who exactly would pick up a man in a speckled tweed suit and yellow flip-flops was a question we turned over for a while. Especially once you factored in that the professor had one of those unchecked beards you see on nuts who live in caves or trees. Big Dan was the only one among us who still picked up strangers sometimes, and that was because he liked an audience, got bored talking to himself.

Once he'd stopped for a boy up near the river who was so monumentally rank that Big Dan ended up having to sell his car, and even that didn't break him of the habit.

So we deferred to Big Dan as our resident authority on hitchhikers, but once he'd gotten a look at Reginald Duff, Big Dan told us, "Not a chance."

We saw the professor around because Kandy finally took charge of him. She got him a room at the Laurel Lodge, the one right next to hers, and every night she'd pull the glider in front of his door to keep him in. He wasn't about to fit through his skinny bathroom window. She bought him fresh clothes at the big lots or somewhere, a pair of copper-colored coveralls and loafers that he could wear while his flip flops were soaking in bleach and his suit was out getting Martinized.

Nathan pulled duty with the man as well. The professor would follow him like a dog on all the weird routes Nathan had to take because he was emotionally constipated. We'd see them trudging here and there, and while you couldn't really talk to Nathan, we discovered we could chew the fat a bit with the professor.

We'd say something to him about the fine weather we were having, and he'd tell us, "Purity of heart is to will one thing," or something like it.

If he'd ever stayed up at Eaglesworth, we sure couldn't get him to say, and none of us around remembered ever seeing the man before. We went through the snapshots Kandy had given us to try to pick him out. There were assorted children pictured, aside from Ken in his striped shirt and the girl on the dog we'd all decided was Nellie, but it was hard to say if any of them had grown up to be Reginald Duff. He was such a lumbering, hairy thing he hardly looked to have ever been a child.

Kandy, of course, hauled him up to Eaglesworth to try to draw him out that way. She got Rick from Galveston's permission to walk the professor all over the place, so we'd see them down where the ponds used to be or up in the poplar grove. Sometimes they'd walk up and down the driveway, talking. The professor was a wandering sort and clearly preferred to be on the move.

Of course, they went all through the house as well. The tradesmen up there told us about it, especially the paint crew because the professor kept dragging his hands along the walls.

"Hell, man!" they'd bark at him and get something philosophical back.

Reginald Duff sure seemed to know the house. We heard that from Deputy Doby who'd heard it from Glenn who'd gone up with Kandy and Reginald Duff a time or two.

"Knows it how?" We put that to Glenn himself. He waved us off at first but told us what we wanted in due time. Glenn was a blurter and could only put off telling you what he knew, could never keep from doing it entirely.

We learned from him that Reginald Duff had hung around Eaglesworth as a child. Glenn didn't know just when or why or how, which meant maybe the professor couldn't remember or Kandy had declined to tell him because she'd noticed that everything Glenn knew had a way of getting out. When Glenn could give us nothing further, we started working on Rick from Galveston's tile man instead.

He was staying out at the Day's Inn, had come clear over from Norfolk because he did some special kind of work that Rick felt he required. The guy made pictures out of shattered bits of tile — flowers and horses and hillsides, like that — so he'd built kind of a reputation as a kitchen backsplash and tub surround artist, but we only ended up knowing him as a chatty drunk.

He'd come into The Anvil about every night to have six or eight longnecks and try to make inroads with Randi, but he was fairly pathetic at it. He kept talking fishing with her and telling her stories of stuff he'd caught. He'd describe the boat he went out in, the size of the motor, like that.

We finally lured him to our table after he'd gotten smacked down by Randi. He tried to slip her the key card to his Day's Inn room, and Randi told him that was a no-damn-way sort of thing. Long years of experience had taught Randi to let men down gently at her peril because we'll find encouragement in places where no woman would think to look. So she barked at the boy and bit him both, stung him even six beers in, and we waved him over so we could explain to him how Randi worked.

"Be worse if she went off with you," we told him. "She's powerfully hard on men."

He went slack and contemplative. We bought him a fresh longneck. "Got a girl back home," he said, "but she ain't here." Then we heard about his outboard motor and a channel bass he'd caught.

"They say funny stuff's going on at the house?" We let Edgar start in because he has one of those naturally friendly faces.

"Big dude in the suit?" that tile boy asked, and we all nodded back.

"You hear about the box of toes?"

He told Edgar that he had and how they'd found a picture up in the fireplace of the queen or something. "Funny spot for it, don't you think?"

Then we gave him the story of Eaglesworth. The Avent history. The Crawley-Lowells, and Frank and Adelaide's brief tenure until Frank got diagnosed. We told him about the guy from Idaho with the bones and dead Nellie who'd been dug up just to see about her toe.

Once we'd left him a slot for it, that tile man saw fit to ask us, "Is this what y'all sit around and do?"

Then he took the beer we'd bought him and carried it over to the bar. He'd decided, apparently, that even Randi, with her contempt and her half-buttoned shirt was better company than us with our Eaglesworth enthusiasm.

"What's with them?" the tile boy ask Randi.

We heard Randi hoot.

We were stuck pretty much with the facts that came our way, and some of them weren't significant or reliable either one, but they were all that was available to us since we were outside looking in. We'd ask the odd question of Kandy or Glenn, but chiefly we dissected and processed. That's kind of what sitting in a bar is about once you get past the beer and the party mix.

So we weren't ashamed that Rick's tile boy from Norfolk thought we were trifling fools because at that moment he wasn't altogether wrong. What he'd seen us at is what we mostly sat around and did, and there were stretches when it was productive work due to ample grist and times when we were just grinding the flour again. During the tile boy's stay, we were suffering through a patch of considerably more outflow than input. We were generating our customary volume of speculation but were having to build it on tired assumptions and stale facts.

Nobody was feeding us anything useful, but then we caught a break. Reginald Duff decided he'd rather not follow Nathan one evening. As we came to understand it, the professor had trailed Nathan out of the annex like usual and had traveled behind him along their customary route around the post office before the professor got a wild hair and broke off for a stroll. If Nathan had been a normal guy, he would have chased him down and snagged him, but Nathan was far too puckered up and obsessive-compulsive for that.

He couldn't even yell like a normal man would since that would bring attention to him, and he'd likely have to explain himself to people he didn't know. So Nathan took the only course of action he could manage. He pulled out his phone and called up Kandy who was off for the night. She was having dinner at The Embers, a local sour cream dispensary that happens to charbroil steaks.

Some way or another, the professor decided to blunder into The Anvil, which supplied us our first occasion to talk to the man at any length. He was wearing his fuzzy tweed suit and the loafers Kandy had bought him, so he might have looked ordinary but for that wild beard of his. It was thick and gray and reached from his eye sockets clear down to his sternum. You couldn't see skin through it anywhere. The thing was effectively a pelt.

We noticed straightaway that Reginald Duff was not so far gone in the head as to be immune to the pull of Randi and her half-buttoned blouse.

"How one encounters reality is a choice," he said to her freckled cleavage.

One way or another, that woman hears quite a lot of philosophy, so she just nodded and told the professor back, "All right."

"Language is the house of being." He was on a Heidegger jag. "In its home man dwells."

"What are you having?"

The professor pointed at a bottle on the bar back. "And a splash."

That's the thing. He was in there. You just had to work to reach him, and it was precisely the sort of job we do in the general run of things. Once Randi had poured his scotch, he patted his pockets and shook his head.

"We learn from history," he said, "that we do not learn from history."

Before she'd give a drink away, Randi would throw it in your face or dump it in the sink, so we weighed straight in and told her, "We've got it."

The professor showed his gratitude by turning our way and raising his glass. "To the wicked," he said, "everything serves as a pretext."

We had a chair for him and shoved it out. The professor wandered over and sat. He hit us at first with philosophical nuggets that we nodded about and endured, but once he'd drained his scotch and we'd refilled it, he became almost responsive.

"Hear you've been up to Eaglesworth." Edgar again.

He nodded. We gave him the time and space to carry on if he liked, and that's just what he did.

He'd throw in the odd philosophical bauble, but primarily Reginald Duff described the property to us from the outer edges working his way in. We found out he'd had experience of Eaglesworth as a child. He talked about playing in the poplar grove and hiding behind the attic knee wall.

"Any of your people Lowells or Crawleys?" we asked him.

"The comfort of the rich," he told us back, "depends upon an abundant supply of the poor."

We took that for a "probably not", which was kind of how the whole conversation unspooled for us going forward. He'd tell us stuff directly, or he'd respond to us aslant, and we'd try to figure out what we were hearing before he'd moved on to the next thing.

It became clear to us that the professor's family had worked up at the house. At first it sounded like his father, but it turned out instead to be an uncle on his mother's side. Sanford, we'd find out, who had a scar on his chin from El Alamein.

"All knowledge," the professor declared, "degenerates into probability."

Then we learned from him that his Uncle Sanford had been a groundsman up on the hill. Less a gardener than a man who tended the various trees and meadow grasses and was in charge of manicuring the boxwood maze.

"So he'd take you up there to run around?"

That question set the professor thinking, or seemed anyway to cause him to cast back on mischief he'd gotten into as a boy. Maybe up at Eaglesworth or maybe just more generally. He sat and sipped and grunted and was looking altogether lost in the past when Kandy came in a lot harder and louder than she usually did.

"Jesus!" she said once she'd located the professor in the dusty gloom of The Anvil. That was directed at us quite plainly and not in a peace-be-upon-you sort of way.

She'd charged across and was nearly to us when the door swung open again, and in came Gail from the Dollar Tree who we hardly recognized. She was out of her green apron and dressed in the sort of clothes you'd wear to the bank if you wanted to seem loan-worthy. That was a huge improvement on Gail's usual sweatshirt and dungarees.

It took us a moment to realize that Gail and Kandy were together. The way we figured it later, Kandy had probably asked Gail to wait outside, and Gail even had done that for about thirty seconds before she'd changed her mind.

So Gail came on in. Kandy saw her and exhaled in a way that told us everything we needed to know.

Even Reginald Duff must have noticed because that's when he saw clear to announce, "Nature never deceives us. It is we who deceive ourselves."

Kandy grabbed the professor by his coat sleeve. We all waved and said, "Hey, Gail," and decided to leave it at that.

They all three went out and left a bit of a vacuum in the place. You couldn't hear much of anything but the pitch count on TV. We were collectively rattled and more than a little ashamed, couldn't figure how we'd failed to know that Kandy and Gail were an item. It was like finding out your dachshunds spent their weekends playing golf after you'd told everybody they were at home on the couch asleep.

"Didn't you used to date Gail?"

Roland had put it to Dennis, and we all knew that Dennis had squired her around for the best part of a year.

Dennis knew we knew, but since he couldn't call up any Schopenhauer, Dennis just waited for about a quarter minute before he said back, "No."

~~~~~~

It wasn't our business what Kandy got up to, which side of the boat she put her oar in, but we couldn't help but wonder exactly what she'd seen in Gail. Or better still, how she might have seen it given the frump Gail had become. Sweatshirt and jeans and sneakers, hair drawn back and with a rubber band. At the Dollar Tree, Gail was usually moderately grubby as well.

It would be quite the thing to go in that store, get a load of Gail, and tell yourself, "I'll have me some of that."

It should be said that what we know about lesbians is fanciful and from the internet. So we're aware that they're lanky and usually blonde and up for plenty with each other until some guy with stubble and acute abdominal definition shows up. We couldn't locate Gail in any of that, not really Kandy either, and we had to wonder if some sort of frequency passed between real lesbians, something that worked like a high sign so they'd all see past the clutter and know who each other was.

A woman will glance at a man, and he'll decide, "She gets me," when maybe she just caught a whiff of his sour funk, but Kandy had stood there buying knock-off Cheez-Its and fake Fig Newtons while pulling somehow a useful read on Gail.

We were a curious crew, and gay studies factored in, but it was a bit like particle physics for us, and we knew being dim and inquisitive would only carry us so far. So we didn't try to hash out the lesbian mechanics of what Kandy and Gail might be getting up to, didn't even talk about it much as a general concession to Dennis who hadn't been out with Gail in a few years but still took the Gail/Kandy thing pretty hard.

Every now and then Dennis would chime in with some Gail detail that was nagging at him. "When we did it," he told us, "I don't recall her acting one particular way or another."

"She didn't scream Cheryl or something did she?" It was hard to head off Roland.

"The wife just lays there too," Dennis said.

So Kandy and Gail had a thing, and we ended up deciding we preferred a lesbian investigator to one who was just a big, lumpy regular girl. We figured she'd have more savvy and be open to rangier stuff.

To that end, we kept giving Kandy possible suspects to consider, and one in particular snagged her interest. He was old and bedridden and not remotely in his proper mind, so she couldn't get much of a read on him beyond the details we'd shared with her, but he was under the care of one of his sons who set off Kandy's creeper alarm.

We didn't know the boy. He lived out Ruckersville way, two entire counties over, but his daddy had been a bricklayer the Crawley-Lowells had hired out. He rebuilt a couple of chimneys for them up at Eaglesworth and did the brickwork on a breezeway that connected the old library to the conservatory out back. He was a Dudley, that man, and went mostly by Yank back in the day. He could pass for ordinary and polite in most circumstances, but anybody who riled him learned dead quick he had a vile disposition underneath.

He stayed close while he worked for the Crawley-Lowells, rented a room in town and barked up against a lot of local people. He didn't drink that anybody knew of, and he carried around a dog-eared Bible that fit in the hip pocket of his dungarees. When he thought you required it, he'd pull the thing out and shake it under your nose while he told you something dire and apocalyptic. If that didn't work and you were a guy, he'd offer to smite you as well. Women he just shook hard. Children too.

Given all you had to put up with, he must have been one hell of a bricklayer, and he certainly wasn't the only angry Christian we used to have around, but that Dudley made a special impression because he also collected human teeth. He had a pouch full of them, a cowhide sack that he'd pull it out and uncinch while telling you usually a snatch of Scripture followed by, "Look here."

Nobody knew where got them. He still seemed to have most of his, and they weren't baby teeth in that sack but big old grown-up molars. We decided he was some kind of country dentist, though when you'd ask him about it, he'd never come out and say if he wasn't or was.

He was a nut with a trade, and people were often both loose and loopy back then. It was what we had instead of lesbians at the Dollar Tree. You could be certifiable and a first-class cement finisher and get just about all the work you'd ever need. Partly the Bible but mostly the teeth was why we put Kandy on him, and she rode out to see him once Nathan had tracked him down in Ruckersville, but the man was gone in the head and beyond even taking regular food.

His son, however, proved weird and angry and made enough of an impression on Kandy to cause her to quiz him at some length. The way we heard it, he was anti almost everything, the government in particular, so he had no use for a woman with a badge who'd shown up kind of out of the blue.

Apparently, he was surly with Kandy. That was his general way with people. He'd close on them hard, come stalking up, and usually they'd retreat. That didn't fly with Kandy, though, who just found a chair and sat.

His name was Walter Dudley, and once Kandy wouldn't be bullied, he parked himself across the room and glared at her for a while. She asked him about his daddy's history up at Eaglesworth and soon got around to the sack of teeth and the sulfurous Bible verses, gave Walter Dudley the chance to explain what sort of whack job his daddy had been.

He didn't turn out to be much help on that front because he largely stuck with glaring and, when pressed, would throw in a libertarian sentiment or two. So Kandy stayed a half an hour and then called Nathan and had him pull records on Walter Dudley who had criminal trespass in his history and some domestic violence. He'd punched his sister and kicked his wife, so Kandy went to visit them.

Walter Dudley's offenses all came on Thanksgiving of '96 when he was drunk on Drambuie, and the ex-wife and sister both assured Kandy that Walter was too dumb to be dastardly, which they wouldn't begin to say about his daddy. The ex-wife spat once Yank's name came up. The daughter smiled and told Kandy the devil would take him soon enough. When Kandy came back from Ruckersville, she showed up in The Anvil and set us up with Randi for a round by way of thanks because sometimes a pack of busybodies is just the tool you need.

So Kandy had kind of a suspect and Kandy had kind of a girlfriend and Kandy had kind of a nosy braintrust whenever she wanted advice. Kandy had brought out Nathan a little, and she was working to bring out Reginald Duff. Gail, though, didn't seem much different to us aside from her new sneakers, which she must have picked up to wear around the quarry path with Kandy.

For our part, we were starting to cobble together a sort of Eaglesworth story, a two-paragraph version that would fit neatly on a plaque. We'd be more thorough and colorful in the brochure we'd make available around town once Kandy had established a motive for Yank Dudley. We were hoping for something beyond just King James poisoning and nuts.

But then we got a fresh wrinkle when a carpenter's helper went on a crawl underneath the breezeway to see how the joists and braces were holding up. His boss was local and particular, not the sort of carpenter to throw up stick built houses but the kind that worked repairs on historic homes and made chairs and bedsteads and dining room tables in his woodworking shop. He had three lads working with him, all more apprenticed than simply hired, so the one under the breezeway hadn't lost a bet or anything. He was slight and fit best between the lattice panels, so he'd eased in and they'd handed him a light.

He crawled almost the length of the breezeway, checking the beams, calling out what he was finding, and he was over halfway to the far end when he cut loose with a yelp.

There was a guy working on the guttering and another one laying footings for a sidewalk, and they tried to decide between them if that boy had run into a snake or a skunk.

His boss called to him through the latticework, and by then the boy had gone dead soprano. He was yodeling in a way that didn't make a lot of sense, except maybe to the gutter man and the sidewalk footing guy who dropped the skunk and went with anaconda.

2

The gentleman was entirely dead, just not completely
buried, and the carpenter's boy crawled up on him unprepared
for the sensation of bony knuckles prodding him from below.
He was eyeing the breezeway underbracing and poking the
joists with a screwdriver. He didn't want to let one pass because
it looked fine but was soft.

That boy was eyeball to eye socket with that corpse before
he realized what was what, so most anybody probably would
have howled. Good on him that he managed to keep from
evacuating, and he scuttled over the body onto a patch of damp
ground where it was just him and a four-foot black snake, which
he made some further noise about.

The law they got initially was Deputy Rachel and Clark
somebody, a new trainee, and Rachel heard the carpenter out
and then suffered some input from the gutter man and the

sidewalk footing guy before she handed Clark her flashlight and instructed him, "Go have a look."

Clark was a millennial who used hair product in a way that made him look like he was hanging upside down. He was only trying out law enforcement, was angling to be some kind of wealthy something. He'd not yet zeroed in on exactly what. He certainly wasn't anxious to go crawling under a breezeway. You don't slather on as much mousse and fixer as Clark and have any appetite for dirt.

When he didn't move, Deputy Rachel asked, "What?"

"Under there?" He pointed at the muddy way in, which was the muddy way out as well.

Rachel nodded. She wasn't about to go. Mud. Corpse. Snake. Agitated carpenter's helper. This was precisely the situation the Lord made trainees for.

Instead of flopping and crawling, Clark instead told Rachel, "I don't know."

She pointed at the opening. Clark weighed his options, and that's when Kandy came around the house and announced that the state police were taking over. Word was she did it the Kandy way by barking, "Don't touch shit."

She had her flashlight out and her jacket off and was under that breezeway up to the ankles before Deputy Rachel could get near enough to Clark to reach over and mess up his hair.

"Stay put," they all heard Kandy tell the carpenter's boy who was stuck on the high side of the corpse and the low side of the black snake, so staying put was about his only move.

Kandy nearly crawled across the dead guy as well because he was just barely surfacing out of a trench, to judge by the photos of him, and he was so shrunken and shriveled as to be in the neighborhood of mummified. So there was no gore or anything like it. The dead man was even wearing a fancy suit. It might have been foul and rotted in places, but he was clearly making an effort.

Kandy played her beam on him and studied him close before she sighed and grumbled.

"What is it?" the carpenter's boy asked her.

"Looks like he's got all of his teeth."

By then that boy was probably wondering who'd drugged his Vienna sausages since this wasn't the day he'd banked on, wasn't a day like any he'd known.

Rick from Galveston had seen out a window a lot of folks just standing around, and he came out meaning to ask what he was paying for exactly when the gutter man pointed at the breezeway and told him, "Dead guy under there."

Rick swung around and went straight back into the house where he probably had a dram or three.

Kandy had them tear off a run of lattice, and then she crawled out with the carpenter's boy and gave Rachel and the trainee instructions on tools she might have use for and the sort of lighting she'd need. That would have been a thing to see since Rachel wasn't good with instructions and greeted each day believing it was enough to simply be one fourteen.

It almost certainly didn't help that Clark was full of yes m'ams and absolutelys. He made notes on a proper police pad and even tried to use his shoulder mic before Rachel threatened to strangle him with the curly cord or maybe take his exfoliator.

Kandy made a call to a proper forensic colleague. She knew the clinic out by the interstate wouldn't be much use for this, and then she quizzed the workers on the scene who relived the episode for her, and she located Rick upstairs in an empty bedroom that was patched and ready but hadn't been painted yet. He was sitting on a plastic tub drinking Wild Turkey from a juice glass.

Kandy was filthy already from the crawling she'd done, so she sat straight down on the floor.

"What do you know about this place?" she asked Rick.

The two of them had largely dealt together on immediate particulars. Giblets and snapshots, a curly maple box. Our crew had filled her in here and there on what we knew of Eaglesworth, and the historical society ladies had Jamestowned her half to death, while Nathan back at the annex was assembling dates and data. Nobody, though, had acquainted her yet with the yarns about the estate. We'd tried to, but she'd cut us off and pressed us on the facts.

Once, however, you've found little toes in the wall along with old snapshots of folks tacked up all over and then a dead man under the breezeway who looked to have been there for many years, you can't help but wonder generally what kind of place that house might be. So Kandy was hoping, even belatedly, to get a sky-high view of the property from Rick.

"They say your aunt and uncle bought it."

"Second cousins," Rick informed her. "Adelaide anyway."

"You ever visit back then?"

Rick told her he'd just seen pictures and detailed the few improvements they'd made before Frank got his bad news and they'd decided to go back home.

"What have you heard about the history of the place?" Kandy asked him. For her part, she was well versed in the sorts of details that Nathan could turn up on the internet, which weren't likely to be complete or maybe even reliable. "What did your cousin say about it?"

"I'll let her tell you."

With that Rick got up off his tub, and Kandy followed him into the room where he'd been sleeping on a leaky air mattress he was obliged to pump up nightly. Everything else was luggage and boxes and sacks and jeans and socks.

Rick dug some kind of journal out of one of his satchels. It had so many stray sheets of paper and so much folded newsprint stuck in it that it was a bulging bristling thing, just the sort of mess Nathan was sure to have a spasm about.

"Adelaide's," Rick explained. "A couple of properties worth of stuff." He handed the thing to Kandy. "I'm not so sure I want it back."

To her lasting credit, Kandy had no patience at all for moping, so she didn't try to comfort Rick or ease his mind at all. "Thanks for this," she told him. "I'll let you know when we're done." Then she went back outside to wait for her colleague who was coming clear from Richmond.

That's the same afternoon we found Reginald Duff roaming free on the landscape. A fellow we know saw him in the bookstore and mentioned it to a few of us. Otherwise, we wouldn't have seen him because we'd stopped going in that bookstore once it went from general purpose to only Christian fare. Even if we'd suddenly come by an intense interest in Jesus, the flinty woman who ran the place wouldn't let you linger and browse. You could go in and buy a lacquered slice of cedar with a Bible verse on it or pick up a fat smelly candle with the Annunciation carved in relief on the side.

You weren't, however, invited to dally. The owner wasn't that variety of Christian. She was a rigorous Catholic from Columbus whose husband had come our way to enjoy his retirement and play lots of golf. She didn't play golf, and she didn't seem a woman terribly interested in enjoyment, so she took a job for distraction at our stationery shop and bought out the owner in time. She'd noticed they sold lots of Jesusy stuff and a fair number of ballpoint pens, so she cleared out everything else, and you could come make a purchase or leave.

Professor Reginald Duff was doing neither by the time a couple of us caught up with him. That stationery woman was having a solid go at him, but the professor was grinning at her and giving her philosophy back.

"He with you?" the woman asked us when we stepped into the shop.

We weren't acquainted with her really, didn't even know her name, usually went with something like "sour old bag" when we'd see her from a distance, but suddenly she needed us since she was getting buried in Kierkegaard.

We greeted the professor. He had on his coveralls and his yellow flip-flops. "Where's Kandy and Nathan?" we asked him.

She was up at the big house under the breezeway along about then while Nathan, we'd come to find out, was fixing himself from a trip to the toilet, which required about a pint of hand soap and a roll of paper towels and loads of second thoughts about how sanitized he was. So Kandy didn't know that the professor had escaped, and Nathan was only just about to find out as we stood in the bookstore and got advised by the owner, "Get him out of here."

If she said it once, she said it a half dozen times with the professor, of course, supplying counterpoint and commentary

"Once you label me, you negate me," he told her.

"What we cannot speak about we must pass over in silence."

"Being entirely honest with oneself is a good exercise."

"Give me chastity and continence, but not yet."

That woman was about as not amused as a human could possibly get, and she would have called the law but didn't want a deputy in her store. So she pulled an umbrella out of a floor can chock full of the things, and she opened it up and went at the professor. Went at us a little as well. The cloth was stenciled over with Scripture — "Seek first His kingdom and His righteousness."

That was all we saw of her as she encouraged us out the door. Then she shut it and locked it just in case we had more browsing in mind. The professor seemed pleased enough to be done with the creature and told us, "To live alone is the fate of all great souls."

"Do they know you're loose?" we asked him.

"If you want the present to be different from the past," he told us, "study the past."

That sounded like a capital idea, so we took charge of the professor and led him on a stroll.

Back behind the old municipal hall that has been boarded up for about a decade because of asbestos trouble and legal challenges hanging fire we have kind of a park that gets mowed and tended pretty indifferently. So it's prone to be shaggy and trash-blown and, consequently, empty. It seemed like the perfect spot to let Reginald Duff stalk around while we talked.

What we'd discovered is you could break him of philosophers temporarily if you caught him in the middle of Schopenhauer, say, and told him with some force and volume, "Naw." You had to let him know you needed an answer and not just a pithy quote.

It also helped that the professor had to watch where he stepped because folks around seemed to turn their dogs loose to do whatever they pleased, so it was treacherous ground for a man in flip-flops, and Reginald Duff moved accordingly.

"Perfect numbers, like perfect men, are very rare" was how he started.

"Naw." That and a pile that looked like it had come out of a rhino drew him up. "Why don't you tell us about your uncle. Sanford, wasn't it?"

The professor nodded as he located a bare patch of ground to occupy. "Heartbroken, he was. Had a girl. She died."

"Before Eaglesworth?" we asked him.

He nodded again. "She drowned," he said, "in the ocean." Then he told us about the current and tides down around the outer banks and managed to shove in a heavy thinker. "To live is to suffer," he said. "To survive is to find some meaning in the suffering."

At least it seemed to be uncle specific, so we let that one go.

"He worked on the maze and stuff, right?" We asked him. "Kept up the bushes and all that?"

That proved to be sufficient to send Reginald Duff down his nostalgia hole. He described his Uncle Sanford to us and told us how he'd been broken for a while until he'd caught on at Eaglesworth. Uncle Sanford turned out to have a knack for keeping bushes and stuff healthy and alive.

The Eaglesworth boxwoods had been monsters, eight footers. It's hard enough to keep little knobby boxwoods under your front bay window without whole chunks of them simply dying off and going to bare twigs. You've got to get the soil just right, and the weather needs to help you. You'll never kill one altogether, but they sure can look like hell.

"What was his secret?" we asked the professor.

He had quite a lot to say about acidity in the soil, and then we let him go on for a bit describing to us the maze itself where you'd could get yourself caught and hung up and think you'd never get out.

That's how it was with Reginald Duff. He could be a regular talker, and you could have a routine conversation with him but only intermittently. He was like a fish in cloudy water that would float up near the surface to give you a silvery glimpse and then sink back out of sight.

"Did you know a Mr. Dudley?" we asked him. "Bricklayer. They might have called him Yank." We had to think Kandy had covered this ground with Reginald Duff already, so we weren't throwing out anything he probably hadn't heard. "Used to carry around a bag of teeth."

The professor looked to be thinking on it, but instead he came out with, "Last words are for fools who haven't said enough."

He wasn't easy, and we were just amateurs at trying to draw folks out, so none of it was pretty and only maybe half effective, and we were still asking the man about molars and getting nothing pertinent back when Nathan finally found us and came as close to the park as he dared. He wasn't about to come in with all that long, matted grass and the stuff it could be hiding.

God only knows how he'd managed to reach us from the annex given how far we were off the routes he usually took.

"I need him back," he said to us from half a block away.

"You want to go with him?" we asked Reginald Duff.

"There is no coming to consciousness without pain."

Then Nathan invoked Kandy as kind of a caution for us and a threat.

It worked well enough. "What do we get?" we asked him.

"They found something," Nathan told us.

"At the house?"

He nodded and waved us his way. We collected the
professor and walked him on over.

"Found what?" we asked Nathan while we still had hold of
Reginald Duff a little.

Nathan glanced around like we were all involved in
international intrigue. "One entire dead man," he said, "in some
kind of tuxedo."

~~~~~~

Kandy's colleague was a Gupta, but his family had been in
these parts long enough that he was Dale Gupta, and he
sounded like he'd come of age in the Brushy Mountains. He was
brown and exotic looking but maybe two-thirds hick as well.

He was a proper forensic technician, very possibly even a
doctor, but most importantly he was a colleague who'd earned
Kandy's complete trust. He rolled up to Eaglesworth in a van
packed with state police equipment that people like him
probably hauled to places where there were no doctors much.
We were eight or ten miles from the county hospital, and we had

semi quasi-doctors attached to a couple of local chain clinics, but we'd lost most of our GPs through the years, and Sheriff Glenn didn't have anybody much to call on who could tell him anything about dead people except that they were, you know, dead.

So it seemed to us that a proper forensic technician was overdue, even before the corpse under the breezeway, since Kandy was having to send off and wait for all of her gee-whiz lab results. Dale Gupta had most of that stuff in his truck, and he sounded like he'd just piled off his tractor, so we decided not to care that he smelled like cumin and was brown.

The way we heard it, he rated a hug from Kandy when he finally reached the hilltop, and she gave him a cooked down version of what stuff had been going on before walking him around to the bit of breezeway where she'd spread a tarp and set up lights.

"Fresh one?" Gupta asked her as he slipped into his paper jumpsuit.

Kandy shook her head. "All dried up."

Gupta had crawled about halfway under when Kandy informed him, "We're pretty sure the snake's gone."

He took some flash photos under the breezeway and collected and bagged whatever he needed before he had Kandy recruit some guys to serve as a moving crew, and they helped Dale Gupta shift the body out of its trench and onto the flattened tarp.

It came apart in a spot or two, which turned those bold boys a bit less bold while the dead guy just laid there seeming monumentally out of place. That's the way we heard it. You had your tools and your tradesmen and your tradesmen's helpers and a dried-up corpse in a fancy suit.

And not just any suit. It was trainee Clark who pointed and told anybody who cared to know it, "That's a morning coat."

Rachel wasn't too pleased about Clark speaking up, so she weighed in with her own view. "Looks like prom rental," she said. "Didn't one of those boys go missing?"

And that's along about when Sheriff Glenn finally arrived on the scene. He'd been out at the high school giving his powerpoint on the ravages of drug use and hadn't seen fit to cut it short since the dead guy was already dead.

"Didn't you lose one at the prom a while ago?" Rachel asked Glenn while he was still halfway across the yard.

"One what?" Glenn wanted to know.

Rachel pointed at the dead guy. "Homer or Buddy or something."

"Oh, right, Alex," Glenn told her. "He turned up at Myrtle Beach." Glenn had a squat and a close, careful look. "Why didn't he just rot?" he asked anybody who'd care to take it.

"Probably did on the inside," Dale Gupta told him. "Half protected under there."

"A whole morning suite," trainee Clark dared to say. "Vest and the trousers too."

"What would you wear that for?" Kandy asked him before Deputy Rachel could horn in.

"Daytime formal." That trainee knew his stuff, which must have been galling for Rachel, and maybe Glenn noticed she was put out, or possibly it was just dumb luck that he chose that moment to ask Trainee Clark, "Hell, son, what happened to your hair?"

How long do you think he's been under there?" Kandy wanted to hear from Gupta.

"In my considered professional opinion," he told her, "a while."

He then recruited some boys to help him load the corpse into his van, and Dale Gupta followed Kandy down through town to the annex. She even let Rick from Galveston's tradesmen all go back to work, which Rick would have been grateful about if he'd not been weepy drunk upstairs.

Kandy had ideas about turning a corner of the annex into a place for Dale Gupta to roll in a gurney and get to work, but Nathan mutinied when she told him about it. Nathan couldn't be around live people with terribly much success, so you might have thought a dead one would be slightly easier on him. No awkward conversations or thorny office politics, no jolly greetings in the mornings or sign-offs come afternoon, nobody tempted to eat your cream cheese and olive sandwich and your nectarine, but just some guy who'd be tomorrow right where you left him today.

But Nathan proved to have kind of a cleanliness thing in addition to his rich vein of social problems, and he couldn't bear the idea of sharing his space with a dead man whose whole job was to lie still and rot.

Nathan explained himself to Kandy by simply telling her, "I can't." He got some help from Reginald Duff in the form of "The shoe that fits one person pinches another."

Since Kandy wasn't about to make Nathan unhappy, she quickly found a different spot. There was kind of an annex to the annex out back behind the PD. It was cinderblock knee-high with the rest screened in, and it used to be a cookhouse for the county police fundraisers. They'd smoke pork shoulders and chop them, sell the meat with beans and slaw, and year in and year out they'd very nearly make a little money. They found they were better off sending letters begging donations at Christmas time.

Some of the screen panels were torn and busted, and the ceiling fans no longer worked, but the light was good and Dale Gupta sure couldn't bark about ventilation, and he had plenty of room for his roll-away table and all the tools he might need. Better still, it seemed fitting that a man who'd been years probably under a breezeway should finally get his proper post-mortem exam in a gazebo of a place.

It wasn't remotely secure though, and once we'd heard the corpse had gone in it, we spent that first evening happening by to see what we could see. They'd left him bagged but on the picnic table where they used to chop the shoulders, and we all wandered through the back PD lot like we were paying respects to some dead dignitary who was lying in state instead of a man in a fancy suit who'd gotten all voodooed and shrunken.

We milled around. We talked. We caught up with people we'd not seen in a while, and by dusk we were having a spontaneous town party. Trading gossip. Floating Eaglesworth theories. Finding out who was sick and with what, and congratulating ourselves for not being dead in a bag on a picnic table.

Kandy and Dale Gupta came strolling through sometime around dark. I think they'd stopped for an evening's check on Gupta's stuff and equipment.

"Hey, everybody," Kandy told us. She could sure be bone dry when she wanted.

What could we do but shuffle and smile and tell the girl back, "Hey."

We only got wind of what was up with Gail once she'd thrown some change at Dennis. He was in the Dollar Tree buying his usual shampoo and swore up and down he hadn't gone there to see the woman.

"Ran out of stuff. That's all."

We more or less believed him and figured the pull of dollar shampoo could probably be moderately strong.

"You say something to her?" We asked him

"Hey and stuff," was all Dennis would own up to. "Three quarters, a nickel, and a couple of pennies." He tapped his chest. "Hit me right here."

"She say something to you?"

Dennis shook his head. "Blubbering and mess, but I had folks behind me."

Leave it to Dennis to worry about clearing the line. That was probably part of why Gail dropped him in the first place.

Dennis always needed to know how people felt about what he was up to, and it didn't seem to much matter if it was quitting his job or crossing the street.

We decided Gail had just been having a day before Dennis showed up for shampoo and that helping to get her stuff worked out was kind of Kandy's problem, but that's where we had the whole equation wrong because Kandy, we'd come to find out, didn't have much use for that sort of thing. She was a don't-bother-me-with-your-messes kind of girl. She'd come for a job, and everything else was frivolous recreation. It wasn't supposed to mean anything, was just stuff you did between shifts. For Gail, it was the shifts that didn't matter.

We had so much other stuff going on — human giblets, secret snapshots, dried corpses in formal wear — that we didn't have much attention to spare for local romantic hijinks, but we were inquisitive people and so couldn't help but notice stuff. That's what happened when Kandy swung by The Anvil finally to give us a briefing. Her buddy Dale Gupta had been in town for maybe three days by then, and she brought him with her to answer any questions we might have before she started quizzing us on who the dead guy could be.

"Maybe in his fifties," Gupta told us. "Broken femur, long mended. Five eight, five nine, like that. Suit was from a tailor shop in D.C.. Leoni Clothiers. Connecticut Ave. Went out of business in 1978."

"He ringing any bells?" Kandy asked us.

He wasn't.

"Remember parties up there? Dressy? We're thinking maybe the sixties, something like that."

Most of us had been kids then who wouldn't have known a swell party if we'd blundered into one.

"Y'all ought to talk to Lady Wilton." That was Roland's suggestion, but we all saw the sense of it straightaway and agreed with him up and down.

One of the Wiltons, way back, had made a pile of money in some kind of fastener business, a little piece of bent steel with a hook eye on it that everybody had needed for something back in the day but nobody used anymore. So the money piled up but then quit altogether, and the subsequent Wiltons weren't industrious and instead lived on investments that paid. Then they had a problem with a Richmond broker who skimmed and plundered and absconded that they followed up with a few bad bets in a sagging market, and the Wilton bottom line was sort of like everybody else's after that.

The family themselves, however, carried on behaving like Wiltons, and when money got tight they'd sell off jewelry or real estate or cars. They'd kept their grand estate house about halfway to Madison, though they'd sold most of the woodlands all around it.

The Wilton place was called Alverstone Park because the original Wilton had come on a boat from the Isle of Wight so that his grandson could earn a fortune making a piece of bent steel with a hook eye.

"They used to have dances and stuff, proper balls. They hung sometimes with the Crawley-Lowells." We advised Kandy to put her sartorial questions to them.

"Didn't he have fingerprints?" we asked Dale Gupta who launched into a Ted Talk on human dehydration by way of giving us the quarter-hour version of "Not really, no".

"Shoes?" we asked.

"Bespoke," he told us, and we decided to wait for later to figure out what that might mean.

For all we knew, it was the way of pedigreed folks (we were thinking Crawley- Lowells mostly) to shove their dead friends under a breezeway instead of worrying about procedure. In our experience, that sort did virtually nothing in the normal, troublesome way.

We offered Kandy and Gupta a drink, but they passed, and Gupta made for the door while Kandy stopped at the bar for a moment. She said a brief thing to Randi who told her something back, and then Kandy reached over and, ever so lightly, touched the back of Randi's hand.

It wasn't a typical Kandy move. That's why some of us noticed it in the moment. She wasn't Nathan's pitch of constipated, but Kandy didn't tend to be touchy at all. That was part of why we were so surprised she'd managed to lasso Gail because Kandy didn't make social overtures in the regular way of things. She just asked questions and not the type intended to draw you out on frothy stuff but just so you'd tell her what she wanted to know.

"See that?" we asked each other once Kandy and Gupta were out the door.

Brady'd had a thing with Randi that lasted just about three days, the sort of fling that started with Kettle One and ended (for Brady at least) in misery once Randi had informed him he'd been part of an experiment in whether or not she could scale the heights — she called it — with a properly bald man.

The answer, apparently, was no. So she moved on to a hairy guy and then past him to some other fellow. Brady was probably still moping when Randi was eight boys up the road, and now it looked to us that very likely Kandy had gone and turned her. There's a lot you can tell from the way a woman takes getting touched on the hand.

We were aware in our bones that losing Randi would be a calamity for us since finding her favor was a bit like getting knighted by the Queen. Temporarily knighted for sure, and you were bound to be anguished after, but you got to be Galahad for, on average, two days and a half. We knew exactly what Randi going over would say about local men, not that we weren't aware what jerks and fools we were, but it's important to know a girl who half buttons her shirt might take you anyway. If only out of boredom and for maybe forty-eight hours.

Naturally, we had to reconsider Kandy at some length because we'd decided early on that she was a loner and an outcast and had been banished our way by her Richmond bosses because she didn't fit in back there. We guessed that could still be true but for completely different reasons. Not because Kandy was a big, hulking girl with hidden depths and talents, but instead because she was an operator — or whatever you'd call a lesbian swordsman — and her male colleagues in Richmond had found themselves uneasy with that.

Edgar, of course, went straight over to Randi and asked her outright, "You and her?"

Randi did that thing where she can't understand you no matter how you put it. She shrugs and shakes her head and leans ever so slightly forward so if you don't freely elect to quit quizzing her, her cleavage will shut you up.

"This is a bad thing," Ken announced, and Ken hardly ever talks.

He was right, and we all knew it, and we already had bad stuff cooking on several fronts. Most of what we were hearing from Eaglesworth was heading in the direction of poison. What if we'd stood by oblivious to some homicidal nut, and he was lopping toes off when he ran out of guys to shove under the breezeway? There's no glory at all to being asleep at the switch. You want to be aware of the villains among you and help engineer their destruction. If it turns out you sat by clueless, you hardly want that on a plaque.

We preferred to be the sorts of people who'd notice when an entire man went missing, especially one who visited Eaglesworth for a party and never came back down. We consoled ourselves as best we could by telling each other, "Randi'll drop her." That's what we hoped and believed since there was no man around Randi had lost a night's sleep over yet.

We worked on Dale Gupta for whatever he'd volunteer since he was the one directly in charge of "processing" the dead guy (he called it). We nailed down his habits after a couple of days and knew we could find him two-ish at the Hardee's where he always had a chili dog and an order of curly fries, and most days he'd video chat with Mrs. Gupta on his tablet. She looked to be some redhead from back in the Brushy Mountain foothills like him. Often she'd be holding their baby who was blotchy and wrinkled and loudly unhappy.

We'd usually let Gupta finish before any of us sat down, and we'd always go as far as asking him, "Mind?" but we were parking no matter what.

We had needs. He had access, and he was leery of Kandy like we were. "Can't say much," he'd usually tell us and then throw us a crumb.

We learned, for instance, that the dead guy from the breezeway was uncircumcised, which we tried to make mean something, but we were half that way ourselves, so it didn't appear to signify anything worth knowing. Then we learned he had a buffalo nickel in one of his jacket pockets.

"Nineteen thirty-four," Gupta told us and left us to chew on that.

One day we heard that his socks were silk along with his underpants and that he'd been wearing a Chopard watch. Gupta even showed us a picture of it on his phone. The band was half rotten and water had gotten under the glass.

"Pricey," he said. "Who around here might wear something like that?"

"Crawley-Lowells and them," we told him. "How about his toes?"

"Got them all," Gupta said. "Don't really know what killed him."

"How's the professor?" we asked. "Not seeing him around."

"Got him out there helping me."

That was a surprise to us since Reginald Duff hardly seemed the sort capable of pitching in and being constructive.

"He holds stuff when I need more hands."

"Could be he knows something about the guy," we told him. "Ever ask him about his uncle?"

Dale Gupta nodded like a man who'd been round and round with Reginald Duff about all sorts of things. "There is no coming to consciousness without pain," is what Dale Gupta said, and then he wondered if we'd heard about Rick from Galveston's three-legged cat. "He sleeps in the sink," he told us. "His name's Gruber."

We didn't see much of Kandy for several days, and Randi stayed about the same, which meant not especially chatty and close to half unbuttoned, and she'd neither confirm her fling with Kandy nor deny it either one. Randi liked being mysterious and would never own up to a thing if she saw she could agitate you by holding back and telling you nothing.

She'd wink and show you the tip of her tongue, toss her hair, tug at her jeans, and sometimes she'd give you a shot of liquor she'd discovered she couldn't move.

But while Kandy stayed scarce for a couple of days, we did get to see one of her bosses. Little toes in a maple box maybe hadn't rated a visit, but a whole gentleman in party clothes proved enough of an attraction to bring a deputy state police chief out for an overnighter. He had a bad suit and a lacquered comb-over, and he drove a dull gray Grand Marquis that he left at the curb wherever he pleased, worse even than Rick's girlfriend.

He was with us about thirty hours, and in that time he took three meals at Cuddy's, always sitting at the counter. He was alone twice but Gupta joined him for supper that first day he came through. The deputy chief always said grace in that showy way that a certain strain of Christian likes to get up to. Like he was telling us all, "Hey, I'm loving Jesus over here."

He'd go on for considerably longer than a goodly man would have needed, and when Gupta was sitting beside him, he talked to the Lord about Gupta too who'd just sat there with his head bowed and took it.

He wasn't a brown-noser exactly, that Gupta, but he liked to keep from making waves. He had a career and a paycheck, a family he went home to, so if his boss wanted to pray at a lunch counter over fish sticks and iced tea, then Gupta could sit for a minute or so and look a little Christian.

The boss and Gupta talked about Kandy over supper in Cuddy's, and we could hear the deputy chief trying to tempt Gupta into taking Kandy down a notch or three. She was worse than not Christian. She was sexually depraved. So the deputy chief's questions to Gupta about the shape and direction of Kandy's investigation left plenty of space for him to speak of her off-duty exploits too. Mostly, Gupta devoted himself to his gravy-soaked open-faced sandwich. Canned gravy, of course, and if you didn't sop it up dead fast, it would congeal.

Since Dale Gupta was Kandy's actual friend, he didn't tell the deputy chief anything worth knowing about her, but he did go on about Nathan for a bit. Nathan wasn't proper state police, and Gupta had only just met him. Also, Nathan was the brand of weird you felt a need to talk about, the sort of peculiar that begs for an explanation.

Nathan was far too tidy and too unwilling to look at anybody full on, and when the deputy chief went into the annex in the company of Sheriff Glenn in hopes of having a conversation with Kandy, Nathan retreated to a slot between two file cabinets and said three times, "Lady Wilton," and then turned and faced the wall.

Glenn knew to call Nathan on the phone, and once Nathan had picked up, they had something like a regular conversation. Of course the deputy chief was standing right there, so he could hear it all. He learned that Nathan suffered from severe social anxiety, that treatment had been unproductive, and that Kandy had gone off to Alverstone Park to visit Lady Wilton there.

"Royalty?" the deputy chief asked.

"She sure thinks so," Glenn told him.

The woman was grand and snooty even though her brood stayed busy selling family heirlooms on eBay, so some wag had dubbed her Lady Wilton, and it had taken in a general way. Nobody could say exactly how old she was. She'd long insisted she was seventy-nine, but she was almost certainly crowding

one hundred, and she remained one of those women who did
her hair and her face every single day.

She dressed only in back because she was in mourning for
her dear Horace who'd died from a stroke back when
Methuselah was a boy, and Mrs. Wilton got courted
enthusiastically for a couple of decades thereafter, but she'd
apparently decided she was fine with being unhitched and
bereaved.

She had children and grandchildren and great-
grandchildren to keep her company and see to her needs, and
she had a black woman named Elsie who was very nearly as old
as she was, and Elsie helped Lady Wilton get put together every
morning. Elsie kept her in stockings and organized her outfits,
made sure her blush didn't look too clownish, and Elsie held up
her end of their daily squabbles. Those two were famous for
fighting like cats.

Lady Wilton was severely skinny, and her hair was
synthetic and blonde and large, and she managed to get around
with just a cane. Most of us had been plonked with it at one time
or another. She'd come our way every other month or so to visit
her seamstress, and if you were anywhere in the vicinity of Lady

Wilton when she was walking, you were guaranteed to hear, "Stand aside," and then she'd whack you with her cane.

She was a pistol, and we collectively appreciated that about her, most particularly since the rest of the Wiltons were meek and ordinary except for a couple of the trashy grandkids who were in the army or jail. Lady Wilton's sons had to keep in good with mom so they could inherit a piece of the estate, which they were sure to sell if the woman ever kicked off and cleared way.

Some guy who'd made a fortune in the bond market would buy it. He would have read a book about Madison and a few about Jefferson as well. He'd think it deeply meaningful that he could own a property built by somebody those men very likely knew. All the old Virginia estates were getting bought up by banking types who had plenty of money and acted entitled in reliably trifling ways, but Lady Wilton was properly imperious, a Griswold by birth and a Wilton by marriage, and her people had been swell since back when Jamestown was an actual thing.

We liked that she tended to be beastly to folks. She usually came out among us looking like an overgrown cricket in widow's weeds with far more hair than a bony woman needed. You could be as courteous to her as you wanted, but she wouldn't give it back. She'd just boss you around and swat you with her cane. We'd decided if we had a queen on our side of the pond, that's exactly how we'd want her to be.

So we were more than routinely interested in Kandy's sit down with Lady Wilton because Kandy was pretty much her own thing as well. We could certainly picture the setting. Some of us had been in Alverstone Park doing one sort of work or another. They'd laid the foundation in 1810 and spent a decade on construction, during the course of which they'd clearly changed their minds a couple of times. The place was Georgian in the middle, federalist on either side, and some sort of Greco-Roman thing out back.

The late Horace Wilton had been a big-game hunter like his daddy before him, and there were animal heads mounted high on the walls where nobody could get to to dust. So they had a big, cobwebby elephant head and a couple of spotted cats, a gazelle or an ibex or something like it, and a sorry looking alligator or maybe just a caiman. He had holes in him from moths or weevils, and one of his glass eyes had dropped out.

Those heads were in the foyer, and they were all around the study, which you had to pass through to get to what they called the family parlor. It had been the dining room once and was right beside the kitchen, but they'd sold off their cherrywood table and so had room for sofas and stuff. There was a view of the weedy back garden and easy access to the kettle, so we felt sure that's just where Kandy and Lady Wilton would sit and talk.

Elsie would be in there too. She'd be included no matter the topic because Lady Wilton seemed to need Elsie around to keep her sparky. Whenever Lady Wilton got off on a fact or gave somebody the wrong name, Elsie would sigh and usually tell Lady Wilton simply, "Nome."

We felt sure it would be a lively session for Kandy and potentially worthwhile because Lady Wilton had long been a prize attendee at local social do's. Sure she'd casually insult the host and hostess and dominate the conversation by airing low opinions of very nearly everything, but she was a Griswold who'd married a Wilton, and her mere presence conferred a kind of social blessing if you could tolerate her insulting your decor and belittling your guests.

We knew for a fact she'd attended various functions up at Eaglesworth. This would have been back in the Horace days, and she'd drag him along sometimes. It was widely known that Lady Wilton and Mr. Crawley-Lowell once got caught in an indelicate embrace by Lady Wilton's husband. They'd gone out in the moonlight onto the lawn tennis court, and Horace stepped outside to fire up a cheroot and happened to see them.

Horace cleared his throat (the way we heard it) and said to Lady Wilton, "Mother, a word."

It made for a scandal. This would have probably been around 1950, and Lady Wilton and Mr. Crawley-Lowell could well have only been guilty of a nuzzle, but it was a stuffier time back then and nuzzling could serve as profound offense. Mr. Crawley-Lowell was already widely known as a bit of a scamp because he'd been found out with a laundress and then got involved with a preacher's wife whose husband was up at Eaglesworth counseling Mrs. Crawley-Lowell, so whenever he'd come up the hill, Mr. Crawley-Lowell would leave and go down.

So everybody knew he was a rascal, and Lady Wilton could have claimed the man forced his affections on her when she'd only gone out to see the moon and enjoy the bracing night air. She didn't do that, though. She might have been mad with Horace at the time. Maybe he'd been off stalking big game more frequently than she cared for or, quite possibly, not as often as she'd hoped. Either way, she owned up to finding Mr. Crawley-Lowell dashing and blamed a touch too much champagne for putting her out there where she'd been.

She was a fine looking woman and took a glamorous photograph. After twenty years of being seventy-nine, Lady Wilton was all knobby joints and face powder, but most any man would have welcomed a moonlit nuzzle in her day.

Husband Horace was obliged to tolerate that sort of thing since Lady Wilton wasn't a woman a man could hope to check and steer, and it could be that six or eight years of sullen, silent aggravation is what finally helped put Horace Wilton down. Or it might have been the extra two hundred pounds. There were photos of him around too.

So Lady Wilton had been a widow far longer than she'd been married, and though she'd made a lengthy show of grieving, it wasn't like she'd sworn off men. She'd long had kind of a Randi thing going but with a black frock instead of a half buttoned blouse, and she worked her way through companions at a far more stately pace, but she most assuredly worked her way through them.

Elsie would tell her husband about it, and he'd keep the rest of us apprised, not because he was scandalized or much cared what Lady Wilton got up to but because he knew her to be mean and flinty and so had to wonder about her boyfriends.

"They think she's loaded," is what we always told him.

"Yeah, well," he'd say, "I think she's not."

Kandy must have known the deputy chief was driving out to check up on her, but even still (or maybe because of it) she went to Alverstone Park and accepted Lady Wilton's invitation to stay the night. That was before they'd even met, but Lady Wilton was like the rest of us and wanted to hear what Kandy knew about those little toes in that candle box. She also must have been anxious to see photographs of the shriveled-up dead guy in tails since there was a chance he'd been a nuzzling acquaintance and she would recognize him.

Lady Wilton made Kandy show her badge and then made Kandy go fetch her gun, which bony Lady Wilton took in hand and studied at some length.

"You're rusting," Lady Wilton told Kandy and then cut a look at Elsie who went off into the kitchen and came back with a rag and a can of WD-40. She sprayed the latter on the former and took the pistol from Lady Wilton so as to give that gun a coat of lubricant while Kandy had a wander.

Lady Wilton's family parlor was fairly bristling with photographs. Horace posing with a dead elephant, a dead cheetah, a dead leopard, a live toddler, an English sedan. Horace lying in state on what looked very much like a sofa. Horace as a doughboy and as a baby in a smock.

There were considerably more photographs of Lady Wilton through the years, some with Horace but most without. Shots taken on various ocean liners and in capitals of Europe, and there was one of the women sprawled on a beach wearing not one damn stitch at all.

Lady Wilton caught Kandy lingering over it, probably caught most of her guests doing much the same thing.

"Ile du Levant," Lady Wilton explained. "Clothing pas permis."

"Uh huh. Ok," Kandy probably told her. "Yeah."

Then Lady Wilton insisted on a turn in the garden, just as a kind of icebreaker before they got down to the gore, and she took up her stick and offered a bony elbow Kandy's way, and the two of them went out the back door for a stroll.

Elsie stayed behind and had a rifle through the photos in the folder Kandy had brought and left on the divan underneath her handbag. She found chiefly shots of toes with a ruler beside them for scale and then a series of starkly lit breezeway man pics and a few wall cavity snapshots of people not posing or preening but only standing around.

By way of a garden, Lady Wilton had what she'd taken to calling a natural space. It had the advantage of needing a boy to mow a path through it twice a month and little else in the way of chemicals or upkeep. It had once been formal, the Alverstone garden, and highly regarded by the sorts of people who care about such things. But as the money evaporated, the garden budget vanished, or shrank down anyway to the price of a boy pushing a Toro sometimes.

There were still exotic plants throughout mixed in with common weeds, and Lady Wilton would point to stuff with her cane and misidentify it because there can't be too terribly many women who'll lay out naked at Ile du Levant and frolic locally with other women's husbands while still having the time and disposition to care about what's growing out back.

On their second turn, Lady Wilton shifted off of horticulture and had a leisurely peruse of Kandy, all the way up and all the way down. Then Lady Wilton indicated Kandy with the tip of her cane. "What exactly," she asked, "is . . . this?"

We're not sure what Kandy said back, but given our experience with her, she probably ignored the question and asked about Eaglesworth stuff instead, which wouldn't have gone over terribly well with Lady Wilton because she didn't tolerate non-responsive people with any grace.

We'd most of us been through some sort of give and take with Lady Wilton when she'd ask us to do a thing for her — open a door or carry a bag — or she'd inquire after something and we'd be slow to get back to her because we thought we could put off a woman who'd been seventy-nine forever.

Kandy probably thought that too, but Lady Wilton was damned dogged.

"Your style," she said, or something like it. "Explain."

There was no getting away for Kandy unless she wanted to be out there strolling through that weedy garden until dark. Lady Wilton was that tenacious and fully prepared to plague

Kandy about her fashion choices. We'd gotten the feeling from Kandy that she was like a man with stuff like that.

We buy pants that don't pinch and shirts with tails long enough to tuck, and our shoes are all either thin-sock or thick-sock models, whatever'll make them fit. There were guys around town who cared more than normal what they got seen wearing, but they were usually the madras and pastel trouser crowd.

We felt sure Kandy preferred her boots and orange socks for some practical reason and wore fatigues because her hips went in them without much of a struggle. The girlish blouses and sweaters were very likely a sop to her job, and her post-cranium surgery haircut was Kandy's chief means of expression on the order of Lady Wilton's enormous, blonde wigs. Lady Wilton accessorized with pearls while Kandy made do with ear metal, but the more we thought about the pair of them the more we felt they were alike.

That's probably why they got on, or why Lady Wilton ended up confiding in Kandy like she did, and on their last turn through the garden Lady Wilton dropped a nugget.

She pointed out to Kandy her three varieties of hostas and spoke of the conditions they needed in order to thrive, which was probably not swamped by a privet hedge and half blanketed in scuppernong vines, but Lady Wilton liked to hold forth, and Kandy was being careful with her until she grew to feel that the moment was right to shift over to Eaglesworth.

"Did you hear what we found?" Kandy asked Lady Wilton and probably got back Lady Wilton's version of Amory's cue-ball squint. "A body," Kandy told her. "Male. Dress clothes. Half buried under the breezeway."

"Breezeway?" Lady Wilton wouldn't have been big on architectural niceties.

Kandy probably went with, "You know. That thing off the back of the house."

Lady Wilton must have believed she had Kandy slotted and figured by then because she told Kandy, "Ah," told Kandy, "Probably Dwight."

4

Not the supreme allied commander. A different Dwight altogether, and a little less swell than his formal get up had led us to believe. He was a Remington who let people think he was descended from Eliphalet (the flintlock guy), but in fact he was from Remingtons up on Delmarva who mostly kept goats and cows.

Dead Dwight was ambitious and had made himself into an antiquarian appraiser and middleman who was adept at shifting pricey artifacts between his well-heeled clients, and he earned a handsome living merely getting a taste off the top. He'd worked to make himself liked, which meant fitting in with the blue-blood crowd, so he'd learned the habits and practices actual aristocratic people tend to pick up naturally from birth.

He didn't play polo, but he knew just how to stand by the pitch and cheer. What hat to wear when. What tailor to frequent. Which vintages of Burgundy were ready to be quaffed, and how to say "sport" and "rather" as if you'd heard your daddy and his daddy before him say them both for years.

According to Lady Wilton, Dwight had taken a wife he regretted, a woman he'd met at a cotillion who'd proven to be a moderate fraud as well. She was a Weymouth who claimed to have Du Pont attachments, at least she hinted at and around it the way a genuine tangential Du Pont would. While her people didn't raise goats and cows on a Chesapeake tidal farm, her mother had divorced her father who'd taken all the pedigree with him.

"He was a climber, that Dwight," Lady Wilton explained to Kandy, and Lady Wilton was down on climbers. She had this view of the world that people get slotted early on and are best served if they stay where they've been put.

That's kind of why we enjoyed running across Lady Wilton because she didn't consider us layabouts who'd squandered our potential but just folks who'd accepted their level and couldn't be bothered to try to climb. Kandy surely gave Lady Wilton that impression as well. She did what she did precisely how she chose to do it and didn't appear to have much use at all for what other people thought.

They likely had dinner on TV trays. That's what it had come to with Lady Wilton, and Kandy had probably been forced to watch a game show because Alverstone Park had gotten to be one of those homes where the television was always on.

"What happened to him?" Kandy must have asked Lady Wilton in time.

"Who?" The woman had been seventy-nine for so long she'd earned the right to be forgetful.

"Dwight Remington."

And that's when she'd explain one time further what variety of Remington Dwight had actually been. That was the way with Lady Wilton. She'd be crisp and dead on point until she either got tired and distracted or decided to be wily. It was hard to ever know precisely what was going on with her.

"We found him half-buried under the breezeway," Kandy reminded Lady Wilton.

"Bad ticker."

"Oh?"

"That's what he always said."

They were likely eating Salisbury steak, the frozen pre-cooked kind, which is stringy and tough and hard to manage on a TV table, so we figured Lady Wilton had ample occasion for interruptions. First she'd have Elsie bring her a series of ever sharper knives, and Elsie would offer to cut up the steak every time she brought one, but Lady Wilton would snap back at her that she could still well feed herself.

Ultimately, she'd instruct Elsie, "Come in here and cut this." Those of us who'd worked at Alverstone Park had heard some version of it all before.

"Of course," Lady Wilton would eventually add, "Dwight said a lot of things."

"You had a . . . relationship with him?"

And that's when Lady Wilton would take pains to acquaint Kandy with the various degrees of intimacy indulged in by women of her station, which probably started with casual flirtation and worked up in steps and levels to some polite way of saying full, naked surrender. Lady Wilton probably went with "coupling" or something in the vicinity of it because that sounded like something you'd do in the moonlight while a dance band played inside.

As we came to understand it, Lady Wilton had allowed Dwight a nuzzle or two. He was still married at the time and

Horace was dead or in Africa, and Lady Wilton told Kandy that Dwight had talked rot about leaving his fake Du Pont wife.

"Why would I want him?" Lady Wilton asked Kandy.

"Did you realize he was dead?"

"Who isn't?"

"Specifically him, though?" Kandy asked her.

"I knew he was . . . scarce."

That's how we got it from Elsie's husband. Scarce was absolutely a Lady Wilton word because she was sure to go on and say that too few people know how to be it.

Kandy pressed Lady Wilton to tell her about the Crawley-Lowell's, and that was just the sort of thing Lady Wilton could go on at length about, chiefly because the Crawley-Lowell's had been dramatically imperfect. Passionate to a fault, is the way that Lady Wilton phrased it.

"Hotheads. She was anyway. Him too a little." And the woman cataloged for Kandy notorious fights the couple had. Notorious anyway to Lady Wilton's crowd. What we heard of them sounded routine.

The Lowell woman would peck at her husband until he got fed up, and he'd throw a glass or stalk off and be gone for a couple of days. In the interim, one or both of them would slum around beneath their station because they felt wounded and were half sloshed on sloe gin. Then there would be recriminations, reluctant apologies, and visits to the sorts of spas that specialized in monied drunken hotheads.

Lady Wilton did quite a lot of talking and supplied Kandy with plenty of texture, but as we understood it she didn't know or wouldn't say what had happened with Dwight Remington. He was around and then he wasn't, and people decided he'd made a crossing, possibly to Rotterdam because he'd mentioned Rotterdam once or twice.

"And when he didn't come back?"

Lady Wilton assured Kandy people died in Rotterdam too.

The TV stayed on as Kandy and Lady Wilton enjoyed (we'll call it) some sherry, but Lady Wilton wouldn't permit Elsie to spend money on anything decent, so she'd buy fortified wine at the Kroger and pour that into a proper sherry bottle left over from back in the heady days before Lady Wilton was seventy-nine. A little of that kind of dram can go a very long way with people, even big lumpy girls like Kandy who are used to tequila instead.

So Kandy likely got done in pretty quickly while Lady Wilton watched her shows and promised Kandy to study the photographs she'd brought along in the morning, and Kandy went up to one of the musty guest rooms and missed the Laurel Lodge.

Come morning, or rather just shy of noon, Lady Wilton made an appearance in the family parlor where she looked through Kandy's photographs as promised. She'd already seen a few of the Dwight Remington ones, and though he'd aged poorly under the breezeway, Lady Wilton told Kandy, "We thought Rotterdam."

"We who?"

"You know. Our crowd."

We knew what she meant. Somebody would have said Dwight had talked about getting on a ship, and for everybody else that was quite enough to put him across the ocean.

"It looks like one of your crowd might have buried him. Half buried him anyway."

"So . . . initiative," Lady Wilton said, "but not too terribly much."

That must have sounded about right to Kandy. "Remind you of anybody?"

"Maggie had a gardener."

"Is that the Lowell woman?"

Lady Wilton nodded. "Peculiar creature. He was exactly the sort to half do everything."

"Do you know his name?" Kandy asked.

Lady Wilton looked at Kandy like Kandy had charged her to calculate a lunar escape velocity. She laughed a little and told Kandy, "Gracious no."

Breakfast at Alverstone Park was instant coffee and chocolate Little Debbies with pink icing. We were certain of that because Kandy put a photo up online along with a snapshot of a stuffed cheetah so dusty it looked to have just crawled out from under a bed.

Kandy took her leave of Lady Wilton and came back over to us, or over to Nathan and Reginald Duff anyway and her forensic friend Dale Gupta who probably all congratulated her on dodging the deputy state police chief.

We got a visit from Kandy that very evening. More likely, Randi got a visit from Kandy first and then we got one shortly thereafter. She came over and parked herself with us.

"Alverstone Park?" we asked her.

She nodded.

"They cleaned off that elephant yet?"

"Nope."

"Spaghetti or Salisbury steak?"

She filled us in. "Dwight Remington," she said. "Ring any bells."

The name didn't, and we told her as much.

"The Lowell woman had a gardener. Know anything about him?"

Ken did a little. "He used to clip the maze."

"Name?"

Ken shrugged. "Had curly hair."

"See him in any of the pictures?"

Ken hadn't and said so.

Then Kandy got up and left us for Randi at the bar, Randi who worked every night from about three thirty to closing, Randi who handed her apron to gangly Murray who'd come blinking out of the kitchen. She gave him a few last minute instructions, and then damned if she didn't leave.

Even though most of us rarely worship, we threw into together with a plea to the Maker that Randi was out there jumping Kandy's car.

We resented Kandy, of course, for working our side of the street, and we couched it like we were worried what Rick from Galveston would say once, in addition to Randi dropping him, he'd found out she'd gotten poached. We figured he'd be liked Dennis with Gail but exponentially worse.

We'd never seen Randi wounded and needy and so were hoping that's how she'd end up, less for the sting it would cause her than the general novelty. We didn't get out and around very widely, except maybe for Brady who went to Zaire once on some kind of Christian mission and brought back a mask carved out of blackwood and an intestinal parasite.

The rest of us largely stayed put, so our distractions and amusements had to come to us. That made Kandy a kind of local blessing since she seemed prepared to spend her workdays flipping over our rocks, and she passed her nights in the company of women we wouldn't have guessed were bent and tilted. Especially Randi who was a famous serial heterosexual.

While Kandy's off-hour exploits made for a lively, diverting topic, we were troubled by the course her investigation appeared to be taking. Kandy didn't tell us terribly much, but we could see what was going on, and for all of her success in the dark, she appeared to be flailing in the sunlight. She had two dead people, snapshots, and a box of little toes.

For our part, we had kind of theory why the guy under the breezeway was only about half buried because we knew people who'd only gotten sort of put in the ground. There were family graveyards all over the place, a lot of them fenced off on pasture hilltops, and occasionally when grandpa kicked, you couldn't be bothered to treat him right.

We're talking country people here with little use for rules and procedures, most particularly when an arm of the actual government was involved, even the well-meaning, half-witted sort of official on the county level. Some folks just hate to be instructed and hemmed in. So we'd had several local incidents where folks died and the family free-lanced everything after that. They put the bucket on the tractor and went up and dug the best hole they could manage, made a box and filled it, read a couple of Bible verses, and then had a potluck meal. No death certificate. No embalming, and grandpa's checks just kept on coming, which turned into a whole other thing.

It could have been that the Crawley-Lowells arrived at Eaglesworth with some gumption and a clear sense of what was right and what was wrong, but exposure to us had worn them down over time and they'd grown gradually more shiftless until they'd guessed it would be okay to let their gardener bury a guy.

He was only a guest at their party and, in fact, a kind of merchant who'd made himself useful to fine folks but wasn't authentically one of them.

"Do something with him," they well could have suggested to their gardener, and he'd shoved that dead man under the breezeway until he could find a better spot. Like often happens, he never got back to the job.

We were chiefly trying to put together a story meant to make plaque-worthy use of the assorted nuggets we had. Being civilians, we likely weren't as down on people as Kandy had become, which meant we still thought folks got up to criminal stuff for criminal reasons while Kandy had been in police work long enough to probably have decided some people are cruel and sorry just in the regular course of things. They're mean for the pure delight of it and ruthless because it suits them and yet can still get away with looking like everyone else.

For our part, we'd handed Kandy three potential suspects, and she'd taken two of them seriously enough to pay official calls. But the other one was just hanging out there wholly uninvestigated while Kandy busied herself with lady friends and overnighting at Alverstone Park. We liked this guy because he'd put on a magic show at Eaglesworth way back in the day. Roland had communicated with him in a chat room, and he'd found the man weird and unsettling even by internet standards.

"Says he's seen the other side," Roland told us. "Claims to have eaten human flesh."

We reminded Roland Deputy Rachel claimed to weigh one hundred and fourteen pounds.

Kandy had been skeptical about this magician from the jump, but our crew was ready to sign onto something far-fetched. The truth is, we probably wouldn't have messed with him if Kandy hadn't moved on our barkeep who showed us just enough daily cleavage to convince us we were vibrant men, not yet the kind who sat on shower chairs and took lunch through a straw. If Randi had crossed to the other side, we asked ourselves what would her showing up at The Anvil half unbuttoned even mean?

So we were agitated collectively and needed to work out our anxieties, which is why some us took a trip to see this practitioner of the dark arts who lived up around Luray.

We stopped at a Golden Skillet half way so there'd be no chance we'd arrive hungry and eat maybe a dumpling crammed with human flesh, but the guy Roland had been talking to in the chatroom proved to be that magician's grandson who often got on the internet and said all kinds of crazy things.

The magician himself proved little short of delighted to tell us about his career, and his front room was given over largely to photographs of himself in various stage outfits. He wore a turban and a top hat, sometimes a cape and booties that curled the toes with bells attached, and through the years he'd called himself Archibald Rex — Master of Mirage and then Sultan Omar for a while and finally Johnny Wonders.

He set up chairs for us and moved his coffee table out of the way, and his wife — a little round woman who said her name was Dorcas — offered us iced tea and coffee and sticky buns she'd just made.

He put on a show for us and started off with the easy stuff, handkerchiefs turning into plastic tulips, and then he showed us a bedroom shoe and told us to pretend it was a rabbit, and he pulled it out of a box and a hat and, eventually, from his trousers as well.

Johnny Wonders said he'd performed in front of some sizable crowds, and his wife had worked with him on stage back when she was a lot less round. Edgar found the itinerary from 1963. It was framed and hanging over by the doorway to the back hall, and Edgar worked through the dates and locations and asked Johnny Wonders about them. He'd been up and down the east coast and as far west Ohio, and he looked to have played community centers and high school gyms and Elk and Moose lodges, and then Edgar found the entry that had brought us up to Luray.

"October nineteenth," he told us all. "Says here 'Eaglesworth'."

That snagged Johnny Wonders' attention. He gave us a grim once over.

"Well, baby," he told his wife, "I guess today's the day."

THREE

1

"Who exactly," we all asked them, "do you think we are?"

By then, it didn't much matter because those two had been feeling guilty for so long that whatever they'd been sitting on needed to come out.

"I almost gave it all up," Johnny Wonders told us and then looked around at his memorabilia. He'd plainly had an authentic career back when this world had room for a few itinerant Masters of Mirage, when people didn't have phones to look at and every stinking thing to stream.

"Good living?" we asked him.

"Usually. Had kind of a bad spell after . . . you know."

We didn't know. That was the problem. Those two certainly appeared to have unspoken Eaglesworth trauma, but we'd not come — like they suspected — to make them both fess up.

We let Edgar take it. "Tell us what happened." There wasn't an instinctive detective among us. We were just a bunch of retired guys who spent way too much time in a bar.

Fortunately, that was all Johnny Wonders needed. He'd been ready for years. "Evelyn," he said. "That was her name. She told us she was twenty, but I'd say sixteen maybe."

"I had a bad ankle," Dorcas told us, "so J.W. pulled her out of the crowd, had her do some of my stuff. Hand him what he needed. She got sawed in half."

"Up at Eaglesworth?"

They nodded and told us, "Yeah."

Johnny Wonders had worked up there once before, and Dorcas showed us a snapshot of her husband in his turban in the Eaglesworth banquet room.

They had records of every magic show the Master of Mirage had ever put on. Photographs too of most of them, and they even had kind of a picture of Evelyn, the sixteen-year-old recruit. Half of her anyway on the far left of a snapshot that Dorcas handed to her husband who had a sad glance at it before he turned it loose for us to pass around.

Evelyn's hair was piled up in that sixties way, all Final Net and bangs, and she was wearing a clingy gown with sequins and heels a girl could fall off of.

"So she was a guest?" we asked him. "Just happened to be there?"

Johnny Wonders nodded. "But I was the one who pulled her up where everybody could get a look."

"He thinks," Dorcas told us, "it only happened because of that."

Before we could ask them, "What happened?" the Master of Mirage started describing an illusion he used to do, a thing with a dove in a box that had a false bottom to it, and he remembered how Evelyn had giggled when his bird had come flapping out.

He then ran through what sounded like the rest of the act, which had precious little Evelyn to it. But Johnny Wonders and Dorcas had long been show business people and so couldn't help but drama things up. We heard how the performance capped off with the Master of Mirage chained at the wrists and ankles and shoved into a sack that got dropped in a tub, and then Dorcas would toss in a match.

"Boom!" he told us. "Flame. Smoke. Then I'd stroll down through the crowd in my cape."

"Tell them what Shecky said," Dorcas suggested.

"'Marvelous' was the word he used, and he was very big in Vegas."

"And Evelyn?" Better Edgar than Roland who'd been to Vegas once where his wife had won two thousand three hundred and forty dollars playing slots. When his mind ventured west of the Mississippi, that's usually where it went.

"Mrs. Crawley hired us," Dorcas said. "She told us it was a charity thing. More men than women and six or eight girls, probably about Evelyn's age. Drinking gin fizz, all of them. Taking maybe pills or something. Nobody looked quite right."

"Did this girl get hurt or something?" Edgar asked.

"She was . . . poorly used," Johnny Wonders told us, and we didn't get the chance to tell him how little that cleared things up before Dorcas chimed in with, "They were on her like dogs."

Those two might have been swell with stage patter in their day, but they had a heck of a time telling a simple story that turned out to only involve Doras looking for a toilet and opening the wrong door by mistake. She saw two men having their way with young Evelyn. The girl was well out of her gown and trussed up with rope and on the floor.

"Naked, both of them," Dorcas told us. "One on either end."

Dorcas proved eager to supply particulars after years, we guessed, of saying nothing. She'd seen two men and a girl in the throes of what sounded like advanced gymnastic nuzzling. The men were old and pudgy. The girl was probably a teen and tied at the wrists and elbows with curtain sash.

"Gagged?" Edgar wanted to know.

Johnny Wonders' wife allowed for a meaningful pause before she told him, "Sort of."

They'd packed up and departed even before Mr. Crawley could give them their check. He'd been the one on Evelyn's nether end.

"You didn't say anything to them?" That from Roland.

Little, round Dorcas looked desolate as she shook her head.

"Did you tell anybody?" Brady asked them.

"How could we?" Johnny Wonders said. "We were the ones who brought her up on stage."

They seemed to believe they'd made the girl glamorous by association with themselves. They thought if they hadn't used her in the act for everybody to see, she would have gone unnoticed and untied.

"Ever think they might have been paying her?" Roland asked it, but the rest of us were pretty much right there. What was the point of being a privileged cad with salacious needs and urges if you didn't indulge them every now and again?

Johnny Wonders and his wife got irritated with Roland for the question. They far preferred believing in the power of their fame.

"She wasn't that kind of girl," Dorcas assured us, and she shoved at Edgar a sack of buns she'd packed for us to take. "J.W.'s tired. Y'all probably ought to go."

We piled into Brady's wagon and then sat in the driveway for a bit because Brady was one of those guys who never could simply start his car and leave. He usually needed to sit holding his key for a bit while he had a think, and it could be a spot of study about virtually anything, whatever had popped into Brady's head and needed his consideration.

"What's with tying girls up?" Brady wanted to know. "Is it for him or for her? I'm just wondering."

That naturally caused us to do more thinking than we cared to about Brady's wife. She was a nice enough gal but ginormous, and Brady was altogether fine with that. He liked his women beefy and didn't care who knew it, while most of the rest of us went the other way. It didn't much matter, of course, that we were half ginormous ourselves.

"And what kind of knot?"

"Start the damn car."

"I'm just wondering, you know?"

That's how it always went with Brady. You'd only leave a place once you were too put out to stay.

We were all in agreement that Kandy needed to talk to Dorcas and Houdini, and we knew it wouldn't be hard to encourage her that way once she'd heard all that we'd heard, but then three or four days went by and we didn't really come across her. She'd go up the road in her Ford or we'd see it parked behind the annex, and a few of us were thinking of dropping in there to pay her an official call when we got word that she was dealing with a Reginald Duff situation. He'd had some kind of psychic break and was in the wing of the county hospital where they've got security glass and throw bolts in the doors.

We only eventually heard what exactly had put the professor in lockdown from a couple of Harley guys staying out at the Laurel Lodge. They told the story to their waitress at The Embers who passed it along to people she knew, so it went through town pretty much like intestinal flu.

For all his interest in philosophy and his gift for pithy quotes, the professor also had a soft spot for nature documentaries. We couldn't be sure if it was a lifelong thing or something he'd developed at the Laurel Lodge where he'd get locked in his room for hours and have to pass the time.

According to the Harley guys, the cable had gone out, and the professor simply wouldn't be consoled. He just got static on his TV for the best part of an hour after he'd started watching a show about the white-throated dipper, an English bird the size of a starling that dives and swims. It was not a creature Reginald Duff had ever heard of before, so he was watching closely the first few minutes of the dipper documentary when a lady dodged a cat up the road and hit a phone pole with her

Cimarron, banged into it hard enough to knock two square miles of cable out.

Most people would have known just to wait and the picture would come back in a while, but it turned out Reginald Duff wasn't built for patience, preferred exasperation instead. He went out his door and over the glider and served as a spectacle in the Laurel Lodge parking lot. Kandy was off with Randi or somewhere, so the Indiana couple who owned the place put in a call to the county police.

It was bad enough to have a large hairy man out in your parking lot yelling, but it was worse that he should be doing it without the encumbrance of pants. The professor had gone to the trouble to put on his flip-flops and was wearing his tweed vest, but otherwise Reginald Duff was in the world as nature had made him.

Those Harley guys had been around at the time and thought about wrangling the professor, but then Deputy Doby rolled up and made, like usual, a bad situation worse. By the time backup arrived, Doby and the professor were doing some major league tussling in the lot. Doby had used his stick and his taser both, would have probably used his sidearm if the professor hadn't taken it from him and thrown it into the woods. So Doby's only remaining option was to kung fu a half-naked man, and he was making a poor job of it when his colleagues arrived to help him.

"Think he got spunk on me!" Deputy Doby kept shouting while, by all accounts, the professor grew evermore quiet and placid. It was almost as if he'd handed his upset over to Doby by then.

Kandy didn't hear about any of it until the professor was already locked down. We were probably a day late to it as well since word travels around here but not on a timely sort of schedule. As we understood it, the professor kept tearing off the paper suits they'd give him and was wandering in circles around his hospital room on a Hegel kick. "Education is the art of making man ethical" and other stuff like that.

Still Kandy stayed scarce, at least at The Anvil. She could well have been avoiding Randi who turned out to have a few things to say in general about her lesbian experience to a boy she'd decided to cultivate at the bar. He was new to us and very likely also new to Randi. He was passing through on a roadwork job, was some middle management type who never got asphalt on him but just carried around a clipboard and kept tabs on what was due to happen when.

He drank one of Randi's pricey bourbons that none of the rest of us would touch, and he chowed down on Randi's fried oysters that had all been breaded in Bangkok. He probably seemed clean and normal enough to make him desirable to her after she'd tried Kandy the lesbian on for size.

We heard some of what she told the guy, about how she was bored with men and so had figured she might as well see what all the girl-on-girl fuss was about.

"She had that hair and all. No flannel, but a couple of weird tattoos."

That was quite a lot for Randi to say. She usually just leaned on the bar until her shirt had sagged and pooched when she'd try something like, "Up for it?" But she was making an effort with the highway guy. Her couple of nights with Kandy must have worked on her pretty good because Randi seemed to need to talk about it.

That boy finished his oysters and kept on with the bourbon while Randi confessed to another brief lesbian thing when she was in junior college.

"We were drunk," she said. "Kissed a couple of times. Felt each other up. Then she stole my boyfriend and my cd player."

"Sounds like my first wife," the highway guy said, and Randi leaned in and gave him her you're-about-to-get-lucky smile.

She never described what she and Kandy had gotten up to in satisfying detail, but we did hear her confess she hadn't been clear on exactly what to do. "I know my way around a man," she told that boy. "But girls . . ." She shook her head.

Then the guy wondered when Randi got off, and she shouted to the kitchen for Murray, and Randi shucked her apron and left with the highway boy.

"How's that any better," Brady wanted to know, "than what that Crawley man got up to? He liked them young and tied down. Randi likes them any old way."

He had a point. It is increasingly hard, given the world as it is, to figure out just how much worse one thing is than another.

We were still deep in the throes of working through what those folks up in Luray had told us, and like Brady we all had questions about what it meant and why. We'd never known much about the Crawley-Lowells except that they played lawn tennis and argued drunk. We'd developed through the years a middling opinion of them, and now we had to factor in that they were maybe debauched as well.

What if they'd paid for a girl like Evelyn to come around and work their party? Was that just something folks of their class got up to in a regular way?

Was it even remotely possible that the Crawley and a buddy, once they'd watched the Master of Mirage saw young Evelyn in half, only then decided to truss her up and have a simultaneous go?

In the spirit of supplying context, Roland told us about a man he'd worked with who'd either worn rayon underwear because of a skin condition or had carried ladies' delicates in his jacket pocket due to the fact that he was needy in a peculiar way. It seemed even to us that Roland should have known which one it was even though we were well aware that Roland made a life's work of knowing nothing, especially stuff that was staring him right in the face and trying to get understood.

"What did you think of the guy?" we finally asked him.

"Big asshole either way."

It seemed like we needed to decide if the Crawley-Lowell's behavior was on the seamy end of sort of ordinary or as offensive to morals and out of bounds as Dorcas and her husband had decided it was. Moreover, we had the original Avent to throw in the mix as well, especially his habits and circumstances after he'd driven both his wives off when he'd given himself over to orgies and all too graphic journalizing. Add the box of little toes in the wall and the creepy photographs, dead Dwight under the breezeway and Nellie in her closet, even Professor Reginald Duff locked naked in the nuthouse ward, and all of it together seemed to suggest two possibilities — either Eaglesworth manufactured creeps or it was a powerful magnet for them.

We figured we could make either one of those work well on a plaque.

Kandy finally showed up in The Anvil on the second night that Randi had taken off early to have a go with her highway guy. So Murray was working the bar, and Kandy pointed at him as she came our way.

We knew what she was asking and told her, "Randi's back on men."

If that was news to Kandy, she took it well, and she pulled up a chair and sat down with us.

"Nathan said you had something for me."

But before we started in on Luray, we asked Kandy about the professor since everything we knew was third or fourth hand at best.

"He's all right," she told us and tried to get away with that, but we badgered her and pressed her and made a decent show of seeming to care profoundly about the man.

"Dippers," she said. "Never heard of such a thing." And Kandy passed a few minutes telling us how that tiny bird dove in the water and swam before enlarging upon the professor's condition. "Bi-polar or something like it. They're trying him on a couple of meds."

She wasn't drinking this visit. Kandy was just sitting, and she'd given us all we were getting from her where Reginald Duff was concerned. She let us know it by asking us just, "So?"

We told her all about the Master of Mirage, and we mostly let Edgar take it, but Roland kept throwing in with bits and bobs nobody needed to know. Once you've heard somebody like Edgar, who's got a knack for telling a story, it becomes hard to

tolerate the likes of Roland with much grace. So there was
Edgar's Luray story and some bickering as well as we raised
objections to Roland's brand of pointless aside and enlargement,
and some of us were half expecting Kandy to just get up and
leave, but the longer Edgar talked, the more engaged she
seemed.

"You say they had pictures?" she asked.

We told her about the stuff we'd spied on the walls from
the man's stints as Archibald Rex and Sultan Omar and Johnny
Wonders.

"Where in Luray?" she wanted to know. "Do you have a
number for them?

We gave her what she needed and then Roland added,
"They weren't thrilled with us by the time we left."

Kandy shoved her chair back. "Imagine that."

Some of us finally saw her with Randi a couple of days
later, saw them for the first time anyway since those two had
gone off together. Kandy had stepped into The Anvil for a quick
cold one and a Cuervo bump. Randi was working the bar and
talking to her road crew boyfriend. He was a four or five-day
holdover by then, so Randi was pretty well off him, and the last

couple of times we'd seen the boy, he'd looked about like all of them tend to look.

They'd have her, and then she'd pull away and take pains remind them the stuff they'd been getting up to wasn't ever supposed to last. She would have been saying some version of that right from the beginning, but even still the neediness would take hold. It was like they were starving, those boys, and Randi was the only meat they could see.

Road crew guy looked badly afflicted, and it turned out he had a fiancee and even a wedding date, but he was more than ready to blow it all up if Randi would just give him the word.

She wouldn't, of course. That was her world as she chose to run it, and if the men she favored for a day or three forgot the rules along the way, Randi was always pleased to put the brakes on and remind them. It could be she simply saw men as a fleshy means to an end. Each was a tool she'd use until another tool came along.

So highway guy had been getting about an hour's worth of kiss off. We didn't need to hear it to tell what was going on since a few of our crew had first-hand Randi experience. Highway guy was all hunched over and working to make his case, but

Randi wasn't the sort of woman who ever successfully got explained at.

He'd go back to his fiancee, and he'd get married like they'd planned. Randi would be the twinge he'd have whenever he'd order a Blanton's. But first he rated a night or two of misery, and he was having one them when Kandy walked in, greeted Randi, parked herself on a stool.

We were already tuned in from across the way because, as we like to tell ourselves, we're super interested in people. Especially people getting their asses handed to them by girls because you're always wanting to see the guy who's worse at it than you'd be.

Highway boy, consequently, had been providing a service for us, and then Kandy showed up to give the whole business a wrinkle we'd never seen before. Highway boy benefitted, at least briefly and cosmetically. Suddenly Randi was tender to him instead of brittle and standoffish. She freshened his bourbon and laid her hand on his arm while making Kandy wait for her Corona and tequila. Randi tried to pretend that she'd not noticed Kandy had even come in.

It was a fascinating bit of business to see because previously nobody had ever caused Randi to put on any kind of show. She was the steady and predictable one and never pretended at anything, but there she was doing regular theater and driven to it by Kandy.

She gave the highway guy a peck on the lips and then introduced him to Kandy. Of course, he was little short of giddy by then since his evening had taken a turn. Kandy was cordial enough in her ordinary way. She drank her beer and knocked back her tequila and then signed off with Randi and headed out the door.

Randi, of course, went immediately frosty, even slid her boyfriend his bar bill. She caught us looking and shouted our way, "What?"

2

Rick from Galveston went home without telling any of us. We got the sense it was a spur of the moment thing and maybe Randi related. We guessed he'd come out the far end of his Randi fling with a fresh appreciation for his chatty, Texas girlfriend. So Rick bought a ticket and hopped on a plane and flew south to win her back. He was two days gone before we found out or we would have had an extra forty-eight hours up at Eaglesworth.

The lawn was getting sodded by then, and a paint crew and a cabinet maker were still working in the house. The cabinet guy was building some kind of elaborate hardwood closet organizer like a Victorian pasha might have had, and the paint crew was undoing a blue room and retrimming a green one because Rick had picked a couple of colors he'd changed his mind about.

As Barry, the paint boss, explained to us, "You can't tell people shit."

The cabinet maker was some hippie freak from down around Danville who was a hell of finish carpenter but had dreadlocks and smelled like hash, and whenever you told him something, he'd usually say back, "Ski do, man." It seemed to mean yes and no and just about everything else as well.

He'd made a special friend of Gruber, Rick's three-legged cat, who'd left the sink and had taken to sleeping in Ski do's bucket of rags.

We didn't want anything but to wander around and would have maybe felt self-conscious about it, but the historical society ladies were already at Eaglesworth before we even rolled up the drive. And then the postman came and stayed a while. That man is a prodigious talker. And a lady in a minivan none of us knew drove up with all her kids.

Our crew felt quasi-deputized and qualified to visit, and the historical society ladies mostly took pictures of architectural details, which made them seem legitimate even if they were talking gossipy trash. We had kind of a plan, which involved us stopping in every room of the house because we'd caught ourselves quarreling about what was where, so up we went to see the layout and step off the rooms for size.

We started up top and went all the way down, pacing and recording the pertinent dimensions. How many windows and where they were, and we had a look in every closet. The place was transformed from the neglected shell of a house that Eaglesworth had been for years. It was grand again, and you couldn't smell vermin leavings if you tried. Just paint and varnish and fresh trim wood. Rick or somebody had gone through and cleaned every window pane. The place was magnificent but unfurnished except for Rick's leaky air mattress and his assorted bags and boxes of stuff.

We couldn't help but think he'd sell the place. It's not everybody who can go to the time and expense of flipping a mansion, but Rick seemed to have the money for it. There was always some bond market type around looking for an honest-to-God antique Virginia estate. Ours was not in the best conceivable spot as fine Old Dominion properties go. The prime ones are over near Monticello or along the James east of Richmond, but there'd been intrepid souls like our Avent building fancy stuff elsewhere.

We were impressed as we worked our way down from the top, and we make it a general point of not being impressed by much. But the place felt bright and welcoming, no easy trick for a pile of a house, especially one where we knew there'd been toes in the wall and a body under the breezeway.

We'd reached the kitchen before Kandy arrived, which meant she found the tourists first and sent the lady and her kids packing before she had a word with the mail guy and got him gone. She might not have said anything at all to the historical society ladies since Kandy probably showed up knowing as much about Jamestown as she cared to, but she sure enough found us pretty quickly. Kandy came down to the kitchen, and she wasn't traveling alone. She'd brought Professor Reginald Duff and was guiding him by the elbow.

He had pants on, mercifully. A pair of baggy jeans and a flannel shirt you could have put two of him in. He'd stuck with his yellow flip flops, and we all gave him a jolly howdy since we were pleased to see him out of the nut house and all right.

"Does Rick know you're here?" Kandy asked us.

Roland, of course, was the one who told her, "I would if I was him."

She'd turned loose of the professor by then, and he stayed where she'd put him. He had that cloudy, unfocused look people get when some drug has them muffled but good.

"What are y'all doing?" she asked us.

We explained what we were up to, showed her all the measurements we'd taken and told her we meant to draw up a plan. That appeared to strike Kandy as a useful pursuit, so she softened on us a little. "Grounds too, all right?"

That meant we were effectively deputized, and we offered to take the professor with us.

"He'll just start yelling sometimes," she warned us. "Don't do anything. Wait it out."

The professor seemed pleased enough to stroll with us out into the yard, or just as oblivious anyway as he had been down in the kitchen, and we started stepping off the property to get all the boundaries right.

Eaglesworth was best known to us from down alongside the road. A couple of us had done little jobs on the property maybe a time or three, but with that you went in and did your thing, dropped off your invoice, and left. This was our first occasion to just wander around and soak the place in at our leisure. You could see most of town from up top where the big house sat. The flat white roof of the grade school, the steeple of the Presbyterian church, and the AM radio tower across the way next to where the firemen practiced.

We knew about where the ponds had been and the Temple of Luxor too. The old boxwood maze was effectively gone, but there were still four or five bushes at the bottom of the side yard. They were big ones like we grow around here, all of them about eight feet high. They looked like they'd maybe last been trimmed by the professor's uncle, and we were right up beside them when big Reginald Duff pointed at one of those massive shrubs and started to scream.

He made a hell of a racket. The professor had some thunder to him, and he just cut loose and bellowed while we waited like Kandy had advised.

There weren't any words to it, and the man didn't seem scared or angry or anything other than loud. He grabbed a fistful of boxwood and held tight.

Roland's brother's wife had been on head drugs once, and Roland took that occasion to tell us all about it.

"All she did was sit around and eat."

"Jimmy's wife?" we asked him, just to be polite.

Roland nodded.

"Drugs help her?"

The professor would stop to draw breath, but then he'd scream some more.

"Hard to say. Sure made her hungry."

You could hardly hear yourself think, and about the time one of the sod boys came down to check on the professor, he'd decided he'd done enough yelling and went back to just standing around.

"He all right?" the sod boy asked us.

And it was Ken of all people who told him back, "The greatest achievements of the human mind are generally received with mistrust."

We found Kandy in the banquet hall with the historical society ladies, and they were all looking at yellow newspaper clippings that had come out of Adelaide's book, the big, messy journal that Rick had given to Kandy. No sketches in this one, just real estate flyers and pages from newspapers gone brittle. It turned out Kandy had made a promise to those historical society ladies: one word about Jamestown and they were out.

Adelaide must have been some kind of magpie because she'd collected all grades of stuff while she and Frank were shopping for a house. They'd almost bought a place nearer to Richmond to judge by what she'd gathered, but then they'd come west another hour or so and had discovered Eaglesworth.

That was back when we still had a proper newspaper with real estate inserts in it, and it looked like Adelaide had visited the library too and had dug up Avent history. Even the sexy stuff because she'd glued into her journal a sketch of some woman's plumbing, and she had several county property plats as well, so we could see how Eaglesworth had started compared to what it had become.

Originally, the estate had covered sixty-two acres, and that Avent himself had let part of it go to a neighboring gentleman farmer, a patch to the north that you couldn't really see from anywhere. Then that Avent's brothers down by Roanoke who'd inherited the place had sold off a couple of more pieces while the estate sat neglected.

"What are we looking for?" Edgar asked generally.

"Whatever jumps out," Joyce told him.

She still had eyes for Edgar a little. Her insurance adjuster boyfriend might not have been one of those sports fans who'd get all togged up like a fool, but he was probably unadventurous every other way as well. We knew him ever so slightly, and that was all that we could stand, so we couldn't much blame Joyce for still having kind of a thing for Edgar. There were plenty of faults and flaws to the man, but he was enthusiastic in ways an insurance adjuster could never possibly be.

So those two went off by the fireplace and sifted through some stuff while the rest of us enjoyed the novelty of not getting educated on Jamestown as we passed around an article about Eaglesworth that had run in the Times-Dispatch. There'd been a fire, and that was the hook of the thing. A reporter had come over from Richmond and had brought a photographer with him to help work up a piece on one of Virginia's fine old Georgian mansions on the occasion of it nearly burning down.

Mr. Crawley would have been dead by then, and his wife would have been taking in tenants and shooting her pistol when she found herself in the shade. It was a four-column write up with plenty of history, some of it new to us. A bit of it almost certainly new to the historical society ladies as well, but it wasn't like they'd ever own up to that.

That article ran with photographs none of our crew had seen before. There was a picture of the grounds in some disrepair. That Lowell widow had kind of let the place go by then, so the boxwoods were all overgrown, still a maze, but you'd never get through it. There was scrubby undergrowth in the poplar grove. Both ponds were low and scummy, and the Temple of Luxor was actively rotting and looked to be about to fall down.

There were interior shots as well. Fire damage in an upstairs bedroom and one of the banquet hall we were in with mismatched furniture all over the place. More flophouse lobby than grand Virginia estate. The source of the fire was a tenant's hotplate, and she claimed to have been cooking mac and cheese, but the reporter implied it could just as well have been crack. She was that kind of woman, the tenant. He even gave her name, and we watched as Kandy wrote it down in her little spiral notebook. Last name, Morris. First name, Evelyn.

We found ourselves prompted in that moment to tell Kandy more about the Master of Mirage and his little, round wife. We were in the banquet hall after all where they'd put on their magic show.

"Sixty-two, sixty-three," we told Kandy, "and they brought an Evelyn up to help them."

The historical society ladies were anxious to hear what sort of magic we meant, and we let Edgar and Roland describe a few of the tricks we'd seen up in Luray with the bedroom shoe and the flowers and the string of silk hankies tugged out of a sleeve.

We could point out where the riser had stood and where the crowd had been arrayed, and then we described what Evelyn and Mr. Crawley and a buddy had gotten up to and how the Master of Mirage and his little, round wife had for long years blamed themselves.

"There are plenty of Evelyns around," Kandy told us, but it didn't sound like she even believed it. This was the world of Eaglesworth where the people pool was small.

We might have stayed right there and hashed it all out, given the brain trust on offer, but that's when Reginald Duff decided he had fresh cause to scream.

~~~~~~

Dwight Remington's arteries were all plugged up, and he had a substantial tumor, so Dale Gupta's professional opinion was he could have just dropped dead. He and Kandy had a confab about Gupta's findings in the Hardee's. He showed her various results he'd gotten and photographs he'd snapped while he ate his chili dog and curly fries. Kandy made do with just a coffee. She was a Cuddy's girl by then.

We had to think Kandy was fond of Gupta because he wasn't the type to retreat into medical-ease. So she could talk to him like a human and float exotic theories, try the sort of stuff out she'd never tell the deputy state police chief.

It turned out Dwight Remington's dress suit had been made for him in 1959.

"It seems tailors," Gupta told Kandy, "keep impeccable records."

"Anything on Nellie whosie?"

Gupta nodded and pulled up what he needed on his tablet. "Carfentanil. She could have gotten it from a vet. Powerful stuff."

"Suicide?"

Gupta shrugged. "One way or another."

"So you're giving me a coronary and an overdose?"

"Yeah, I guess."

Kandy snorted.

"Come on," Gupta said, "you've still got a box full of toes."

Brady was there and saw it all and got caught by Kandy doing it. When she left Gupta she stepped straight over to where Brady was sitting with his balled up burger wrappers and his cup of watery ice.

Kandy glared at him, left Brady to do the talking. He told us he came out with the first thing that popped into his head.

"How'd it go with you Randi?" Of course we'd all been doing some private wondering, but it would take a Brady or a Roland to it into actual words.

Kandy must have known by then that every little thing around was our business, so she gave Brady an answer, told him, "Made her finish unbuttoning her shirt."

It didn't go as well when Brady passed that story along to Randi, or rather shared it with us and Roland took it over to the ar.

"Listen here," he said to Randi and then repeated what Brady had told us, and Randi picked up the nozzle and squirted Roland all over with 7-Up.

If Kandy was down at all on account of Randi, she didn't remotely show it but kept working the case she had left to her with what Nathan and Gupta could supply. That turned out to be Evelyn Morris almost immediately. She was living two towns over in an apartment building, the kind where everybody's TV is at full volume and Crisco is in the air.

Kandy took Gupta as a way to keep him from going back to Richmond, and because Nathan was suffering through a jangled spell, Kandy gave the professor to us.

"You lot don't do much of anything," she'd told us. "Let him do it with you."

Nathan and Kandy had left a couple of voicemails for Evelyn Morris and had given her a week, but she hadn't gotten back, so Kandy was making the trip with nothing more than an address.

The professor we found ourselves in charge of seemed to be a man on the mend. Not nearly so cloudy-headed, and he had no appetite for screaming. He even gave us a brand of philosophy we'd not heard from him before.

When we first got him, we walked Reginald Duff around just to see how he'd do, and he went wherever we steered him and failed to make much racket at all. For a while, he didn't say anything, but once we'd fed him a chopped pork sandwich, Reginald Duff told us, "There is no other way to find ourselves but in each other's faces."

When he came out with it, we were all half ready to lay it off to a German, maybe one of your lesser philosophers who'd failed to muster much Bavarian gloom, but then Ken looked it up and told us the professor was quoting Rod McKuen who we'd all seen on late-night television in his turtleneck trying to sing.

Got to be the drugs, we decided, and then we got some Ferlinghetti. "Poetry," the professor told us, "is the shortest distance between two humans." Whatever he was on just seemed to be letting the piffle bubble up.

We had three pills from Kandy that we were supposed to give the professor either right before or right after he'd eaten lunch, but somehow we lost them in the gutter as we were walking the man around, and in the course of the afternoon he grew a bit grimmer and more lucid, which we all considered an accidental success.

By half-past two, Reginald Duff had favored us with, "The real world is much smaller than the imaginary," and then a scant hour after that he said, "Anxiety is the dizziness of freedom." We put a couple of whiskeys in him, and he was soon back to his old self.

All this time, Kandy and Gupta were off tracking down Evelyn Morris, which first meant locating her apartment and then waiting for the woman to get home. They were parked in front of her building when a police cruiser rolled up, and an officer carried Evelyn Morris' groceries to her front door.

Gupta eventually gave us the blow by blow, told us that cop looked little more than a kid, and the whole time he was up and back, a woman was yelling at him. His passenger, as it turned out.

Kandy and Gupta just watched it all as the cop helped her up the stairs and then tried to carry her grocery sacks on into her apartment, but she pitched a fit and made him stay outside. She didn't thank him exactly, but she did suggest he ought to go somewhere and learn to drive.

Kandy and Gupta approached the kid as he was heading back to his cruiser, and Kandy did the badge thing.

"Evelyn Morris?" she asked with a glance at her door.

The cop nodded.

"What can you tell us about her"

He said, "Smokes cigars. Lives on applejack. Too damn mean to die." Then he got a call about a break-in and piled into his car and left.

Evelyn Morris answered the door thinking her cop had come back to plague her, so as she yanked it open, she delivered some raunchy abuse. She went ahead and ran out the string, even once she'd seen she was mistaken, and eventually she got to, "Christ. Who the hell are you?"

Kandy showed her badge. Gupta just had a laminated card and he was brown, none of which proved to be enough to hold Evelyn Morris' interest, so she slammed her door and said a few muffled vile things from the other side.

Kandy and Gupta between them put together sixty-four dollars in folding money. Kandy told Evelyn Morris about it, and she opened her door a crack for a peek. She unlatched her screen and tried to get Kandy to hand over the cash for a sniff, but big lumpy Kandy just pushed on in while advising the woman, "Move."

Dale Gupta couldn't get over how Evelyn Morris lived, and he'd grown up in the Brushy Mountains where there were still folks with no screen wire and chickens in the house.

"She had a spot on the sofa," Gupta told us, "and a path through the place that branched off here and there." Apparently, everything else was very nearly solid stuff. Old mail and clothes and phone books most especially.

"It was weird," he said. "She had piles of them, and she didn't even have a phone."

So there was no sitting down for Kandy and Gupta. Barely room for standing up. There was space of an ashtray and space for a TV, space in the kitchen sink for dirty dishes to pile up, and just enough room for a woman of Evelyn Morris' size to perch on the toilet.

"Ever smell a bull in rutting season," Gupta asked us.

Because we were men and probably should have, we all told him, "Yes."

"Like that but add cigar smoke and a little dime store perfume."

"Is this you?" Kandy asked Evelyn Morris and showed the woman a picture she'd dug up somewhere. Or Nathan more likely had found it for her — people standing in the sun out on the Eaglesworth south lawn. The women had on dresses, and the men were wearing suits and hats, and there were two dogs chasing around up by the driveway.

Evelyn Morris squinted at the thing and told Kandy, "I don't know."

"Have you ever been to the Eaglesworth estate?" Kandy asked her.

Evelyn Morris asked back, "Who's he?" Then she turned to Gupta. "Where exactly you from?"

"Around Bristol," he told her.

Evelyn Morris wasn't buying it. She knew a brown foreigner when she saw one. "Outside," she told Gupta, and he would have happily left, but Kandy shook her head.

"Is this you or not?" She shoved that photo as close to Evelyn Morris as her nose would allow.

"Maybe."

Kandy had kept hold of the folding money, and she showed it to the woman.

"I went up there some. Long time ago." She got a twenty dollar bill for that.

"Invited or paid?" Kandy asked.

"You tell me."

So Kandy did. She said Evelyn had been some kind of party girl, and Eaglesworth was a bit of a scene. "The people who owned it were into some stuff. That's what we hear anyway."

"With all the mess they get up to today," Evelyn Morris said, "what we did back then was nothing. They'd wrap a little rope around you and think they were running wild."

"Ever see him?" Kandy had a picture of Dwight Remington, upright and pre-breezeway. He had his hand on something mostly out of frame. It looked to be either a mastodon or a horse.

"Hell, I don't know. They all looked like that."

"Remember a magician?"

Evelyn Morris motioned with her fingers, and Kandy gave her another twenty.

"Yeah," she said. "He was all right. I helped him once with stuff."

"Were you up there a lot?"

Evelyn Morris fired up a White Owl. "Enough. Rented a room from her later." Evelyn shifted to have a look at Gupta. "Like hell you're from Bristol."

"Ever see any violence up there?" Kandy gestured with a photo of the Eaglesworth banquet hall. "Anyone getting hurt?"

"That bunch? They'd just get lit and yell."

That's about when Kandy yielded to Dale Gupta, who didn't much want to be yielded to, but he did his duty and said to Evelyn Morris, "We'd like to see your feet."

They got back later than promised. It seems they sat around a Hardee's and tried to figure out what sort of mess exactly they had. No toes missing from Evelyn Morris who'd complained about her payout once she'd decided she'd probably given them eighty-five dollars worth of stuff, and when Kandy and Gupta wouldn't between them dig up any more cash, the women used her neighbor's phone to call the law.

The same deputy rolled up. He pulled out his wallet and gave Evelyn Morris a five.

Apparently, at the Hardee's Kandy passed a chunk of time in study of one of those Eaglesworth photographs that featured young Evelyn Morris. She was well-dressed and coiffed and smiling, looked to have a life before her other than cigars and applejack.

"What happens to people?" Kandy asked Gupta.

He was working on one of those fast-food milkshakes that's got little in it from a cow.

"Guess things didn't go how she hoped," he said.

On this planet, you could say that about ninety percent of everybody.

"They were quick and neat probably. That's something," Kandy told him.

"I'm still eating."

"Can an old white guy full of gin fizz even get it up?"

Gupta returned a curly fry to its sack.

Because they loitered so and got back late, the professor was about half lit before Kandy arrived to take charge of him. That was the first time we'd seen her with Randi when they were regular again. Mostly regular anyway, though the roles were shifted around with Kandy as the dropper and Randi the drop-ee.

You wouldn't have noticed if you weren't us since there wasn't a lot about it to see, just Kandy the same and Randi ever so slightly diminished.

"Find her?" we asked.

Kandy nodded. "All grown up," she told us. Then she leaned in and sniffed the professor. She wasn't pleased.

"Only a couple of sips," we said, "like you'd give a baby."

The professor was back on his usual canon by then and told us all, "To be aware of limitations is already to be beyond them."

3

Rick from Galveston returned by car, his girlfriend's German coupe and with her behind the wheel. It seems he'd ridden all the way up with Carlton on his lap while listening only to Angie's music and enduring Angie's advice. That's just what happens when you go clear to Texas to apologize.

The first thing Angie did was order the repainted blue room blue again.

It took three or four days before Rick told his girlfriend he was off to the lumber yard and ended up parked on a stool at The Anvil instead. He was well over Randi by then. That's what happens with her guys. She puts them to hard use for a day or three and then drops them and they suffer because they have to watch her settle on the candidate she'll put to hard use next.

In time they get past it, and once they're feeling whole and healthy again, they kind of get back in line. Randi'll tolerate a retread because ours is no town of any size.

We don't blame Randi for the boy she booted who jumped into the river. Yes, he was desolate and inconsolable, but she hadn't done any of that. She was just kind of a box he ticked on the way to the bluff at the quarry, his conjugal visit before he got strapped into the chair. He was going in the river all along, just stopped off at Randi first.

It was far different with Rick. We'd all suspected he'd come back with his girlfriend since he'd gone clear to Texas to make things right, which meant he was a fresh temptation for Randi. He'd returned with a lot to ruin, and Randi was at her best when the stakes were high. We'd seen plenty of it and watched how Randi lingered and chatted with Rick before we sent an emissary over to fetch him back our way.

Rick sat with us once we'd insisted, and we let Paul and Roland tell him that Randi had gone over to the other side.

"Other side of what?"

We explained what had been going on, did it as sketchily as we could manage because we didn't have much of a grip on your real-world lesbian stuff, and then we informed him that Randi was back to ruining men but only on the rebound.

"You went all the way to Texas," Edgar told him. "Don't come in here and mess that up."

That was not our usual line of advice, but we were talking to the Eaglesworth guy, and to the extent that his life stayed steady, he might finish his renovations and give our town the sort of fine, historic home that would rate a plaque.

"Kandy and Nathan have been digging up stuff," we confided to Rick. "Tumors and whores. Master of Mirage."

The look we got from Rick we'd earned — a three-cueball squint.

It was a lot to take in, and we'd backed up the truck and emptied the bed out on him. The girl he'd had a fling with had changed her orientation. The people who'd lived in his house before him had hardly improved upon the Avent. There'd been hard sex for money (probably all over the place) and a magician some guy named Shecky in Vegas thought pretty highly of. Worse still, the dead man under the breezeway had only maybe just expired.

It was a load. We realized that, but Rick from Galveston needed to hear it, and possibly because he thought of Eaglesworth as a real estate investment and didn't have any particular use one way or another for our town, Rick took it all far better than we'd expected and had hoped.

"Hmm," he said and knocked back his Wild Turkey. "Anything new on those toes?"

We let Ken have that one since he'd grown chatty of late. "Out of the crooked timber of humanity," Ken told Rick, "no straight thing was ever made."

Rick had almost certainly never heard a word from Ken before though he'd gotten philosophized at on several occasions by the professor, so Rick sucked on his beer and pointed at Ken.

"Is it catching?" he wanted to know.

Kandy kept trudging in her own Kandy way and took a trip out to the valley in the company of the professor. He'd gone back to being, more or less, no trouble anymore. It seems Kandy or whoever would hand him his pills, and he'd pretend to take them, so everybody ended up satisfied. The professor stopped being cloudy and stifled and almost never screamed, and he could even manage — in brief chunks — the sort of conversation that academics might have with their colleagues in the teacher's lounge.

That would prove convenient for Kandy since they were heading for the campus where Professor Reginald Duff had lately worked. It started life as a high school, and then the new high school got built, and the old one briefly became a community college before the Christian Scientists bought it and added four or five buildings. So if you didn't know better, it looked like an actual institute of higher learning. It was called Parkhurst College, named for some buddy of Mary Baker Eddy's.

Students came out with authentic degrees in regular disciplines, and the freshmen all took philosophy, psychology, and religion at a cheap enough rate to mean they needed the likes of Reginald Duff to teach. We couldn't say for certain he hadn't been a splendid professor, but exposure suggested that Reginald Duff had long been at least a marginal nut.

Kandy had made an appointment with one of the deans but arrived on campus to find him gone.

"Bad tooth," his secretary explained and handed Kandy off to a Dr. Pike. Philosophy also, and he took the professor's hand, shook it, called him Reg.

When Reg fired off a scrap of Descartes, Dr. Pike said, "Yeah," and laughed.

For a philosophy professor at a Christian Scientist college in the valley, Dr. Pike turned out to be a nearly regular guy. He knew his great thinkers well enough, but he wrote mysteries on the side, or half wrote them because he'd invariably get stuck and stymied.

"I'd like to pick your brain," Dr. Pike told Kandy, and apparently that's what he tried to do as he walked Kandy and the professor across the campus to where Reginald Duff still had an office.

"Let's say you stabbed me with a dagger made of ice." That's the sort of stuff Dr. Pike was way too curious about. "Walk me through the forensics."

"Where'd I stab you?'

"Between these two ribs."

"You're dead."

"Yes, but, then you find me, and . . ."

"I thought I stabbed you."

"Not you you. You police inspector."

"Why a dagger made of ice?"

"It's just a thing he does."

"Who?"

"Percival Drake."

Kandy didn't even get to tell him that was an awful poncy name for a guy going around being homicidal because the professor interrupted with a spot of philosophy.

"The tyrant dies, and his rule is over. The martyr dies, and his rule begins."

Dr. Pike nodded. "Yes," he said to Reginald Duff. "Touchè."

Professor Reginald Duff, Kandy discovered, had slept sometimes on a cot in his office. The place was a desk and books primarily with student papers piled up all over.

Kandy switched on all the lights she could find and raised the blinds on the lone window. She poked and scoured as she asked Dr. Pike, "What do you know about . . . Reg? Who hired him? Where'd he come from? He ever talk about his past?"

Dr. Pike filled her in as best he could. It seems he wasn't fully clued in on how Reginald Duff had been hired and referred Kandy to the dean with the bad tooth, but he did have some knowledge of Dr. Duff's past, almost all of it gathered at a luncheon where they'd been seated together.

Apparently, Reginald Duff had been downright chatty at this particular meal and had told Dr. Pike about his childhood. He'd grown up out around Mobjack where his peopled crabbed and fished.

"Talk to you about his uncle?" Kandy asked.

Dr. Pike glanced the professor's way. "You did, didn't you?"

That rated kind of an answer. "He who hasn't tasted bitter things hasn't earned the sweet ones."

"I think his dad died," Dr. Pike said. "Something that runs in the family, and his uncle stepped in and helped raise him. Is that close?" he asked the professor who said, "Sanford," by way of yes.

"Right, Sanford," Dr. Pike told Kandy.

Kandy was quick and careful when she looked for stuff. We'd all seen her poking around up at Eaglesworth. So as Dr. Pike told her what he could remember of his luncheon chat with the professor, Kandy was rooting out every pertinent personal item that Reginald Duff had left behind. That was chiefly handwritten notes on various scraps of paper, and then she found one of those auto mileage books like you buy when you're feeling ambitious and think you're going to jot all your commuter details down.

The first few pages were, in fact, devoted to fuel purchases and odometer mileage, even tire pressure once or twice, but after that the professor had written stuff that looked to have popped into his head. Some of it was philosophical. There were three or four shopping lists, and twelve pages where he'd written Sanford as many times as it would fit.

Kandy showed one of them to Reginald Duff who told her, "Do not weep. Do not be indignant. Understand."

"Spinoza," Dr. Pike said and because he was an academic, he added, "Dutch but part Sephardic. A lens grinder, and it killed him. Silicosis. He was only forty-four."

Kandy ignored him and asked the professor, "Where'd you leave your car?"

Reginald Duff owned a Regal sedan that was dented about everywhere it could be and was sitting out under a maple tree at the edge of a campus lot. The vinyl top was faded and peeling, and even the riveted tin patches had rust. There were three pairs of shoes on the passenger floorboard and a proper dress suit laid out on the back seat. A shotgun in the trunk and a Colt revolver, and in the glove box on the registration was Reginald Duff's home address.

His house was up near Port Republic, a good twenty miles from campus and down an oiled road in a black oak grove. The grass in the yard was knee-high, and the front door was standing open. Everything inside was either busted or overturned. Two corner cabinets had been reduced to splinters, and the dishes in the kitchen had been broken all over the floor. The toilet and sink were both shattered along with every mirror in the place and all the picture frame glass.

"You do this?" Kandy asked.

The professor had gotten as far as the kitchen, and that's where he'd decided to plant and stand.

We'd hear from her that you could see the rage on display if you knew how to look. Kids broke stuff but rarely stuck at it, and drunks left mess behind. What she saw was a bluff impulse for destruction gone unchecked. The professor, she grew to feel sure, had worked his way around the place banging and busting everything he could reach.

She found what she was looking for on the back screen porch, a sturdy cardboard box that had been stomped and kicked around, but it was still a box and had stuff in it along with a shipping label on a flap. It had come to Reginald Duff from a nursing home in Weatherly, Pennsylvania, and there was a sealed envelope among the stuff inside that the professor hadn't bothered with. Kandy tore it open to find some boilerplate condolences from the "Winning Staff at Kirby Care" who were marking the sad passing of Roosevelt Sanford Duff, age ninety-three.

The box held what was left of the man, which is not to say his ashes, but what looked like personal items they'd collected from his room. A Bible, three embroidered handkerchiefs, a watch with a band and one without, a dented metal flask, a purple heart, a framed picture of what most assuredly was his momma, and a stack of other photographs with a ribbon tied around them along with a little wooden poplar box that had walnut inlays on it. Stickmen mostly in tall stovepipe hats.

"So Uncle Sanford died," Kandy said. "Was that kind of a problem for you?"

The professor made a noise, to hear it from Kandy, like a reed bear might make.

"Ok to take it with us, right?" She meant the box.

The professor made a bit more racket.

"I'll put it in the back and cover it up. You won't even know it's there."

The professor stopped on the way to the front door because he'd had a thought. "Men make their own history," he said to Kandy, "but they do not make it as they please."

~~~~~~

Rick's girlfriend, Angie, was if anything more angry than the first time she came. She seemed to roll out of bed irritated and, as her day unspooled, get worse. Or it could be she was just sour by nature and, over time, it concentrated. She was so regular at it that people soon knew better than to be offended. We hadn't done anything to set her off. She'd just shown up that way.

She got in a scrum with Gail, and that's what truly turned our crew against her, and it didn't even happen in the Dollar Tree. You'd expect a girl like Angie to go into a discount store like that and find plenty of reason to roll her eyes and sneer. Everything in there's a dollar, after all, and some of its worth forty cents, and Angie was a girl with a Galveston condo that was almost on the water.

But Gail was off for the afternoon and, the way we heard it from Dennis, she was well and truly past Kandy and was even grateful for the fling. It wasn't like she'd discovered she was a beautiful flower long untended and what she craved more than anything was a woman's loving touch. Gail simply realized she'd steered herself into an amorous cul-de-sac because for a few years she'd done nothing with anybody — not male, not female, not even pixelated. She'd just been putting on her loose, grubby clothes and showing up at work.

Her Kandy thing, then, had jarred her awake in a general way, and Gail had started taking an interest in how she looked and what she ate, and she'd resolved to be more direct with people and tell them how she felt, which if anything had made the Dollar Tree every so slightly less inviting since Gail was likely to ring you up while ticking off your infirmities. She wasn't cruel, but nobody buying knock-off Listerine and Mexican laundry soap wants to hear from the checkout girl, "I'd probably have that mole removed."

But Gail had long been one of ours, and Angie was up from Texas, so when word got around they'd tangled, we were all on one side of it.

Gail was in the ladies wear boutique where the tobacco shed used to be, and she was trying on hats because she'd resolved to be more devil-may-care and jaunty. We eventually saw the hat she bought, and it wasn't at all becoming, but we gave her points for trying to mix things up.

She had the thing on her head when Angie stepped into the boutique. Angie would come into town and visit stores to make sure we had nothing she wanted, and then she'd go back and complain to Rick until they'd gone on a spree in D.C.. So she stepped into that boutique merely to further confirm her suspicions and came across Gail trying on a hat. Nothing dressy, just a lid to keep her head out of the sun.

Gail didn't invite an opinion from Angie, but she got one anyway. "Oh, sugar, no," Angie said and then checked out a rack of frocks.

"What did you say?" Gail asked her.

Angie pointed at Gail's hat, shook her head and scrunched up her nose, and that would have been the end of it if Gail hadn't been emboldened by her brief affair with Kandy to believe she wasn't obliged to tolerate guff from some bony Texas girl.

Gail's never been much of a talker, and there's no reason to think she's a puncher, but she could shove that woman well enough, and that's exactly what she did. Gail knocked her clean over. That boutique is cluttered, and Angie caught her foot on something and pitched onto her ass. Then she opted immediately for undiluted indignation while Gail couldn't be bothered to talk to her further and instead kicked her twice.

Gail told Penny at the register she'd be wearing her new hat home.

She was long gone by the time the police came, and then Rick raced in thinking something awful had happened to his girlfriend because she'd only been able to scream and blubber on the phone.

Penny had been flipping through a magazine, like usual, and so hadn't been paying strict attention.

"They had words," she informed Deputy Rachel, who was mostly investigating but was also shopping a bit.

"The cow kicked me," Angie announced by way of clarification.

Rachel looked to Penny for some kind of confirmation, but Gail would be back in the shop while the Texas girl probably wouldn't, so Penny only said again, "They had words."

Deputy Rachel found Gail clocked in and working at the Dollar Tree, and she made sure to tell Gail Angie had called her a cow, primarily because that meant Deputy Rachel could assure Gail she was just big boned and then stand there being only one fourteen.

Even still, Rachel couldn't get a rise out of Gail because Gail had turned a corner. She was working on herself and wore hats if she wanted, and she'd lately taken to lunching on romaine lettuce as if it were food.

Angie would have been wise to live and learn, but she wasn't about to do that, and she made Rick hire her a lawyer, the only local one we had, who was almost exclusively a deed and contracts guy. He was a Mills from out in the county who'd worked his way through school down in Salem, and his parents had named him Hobart after a washing machine they'd loved. They'd had double-digit children and limited imagination, but we'd gotten a lawyer out of it, and we'd all used Hobart Mills even if he sounded like someplace you'd drive on a weekend for a picnic lunch.

Angie wanted vindication, intended to go true bill on Gail's ass, and she let lawyer Hobart Mills know she would be unhappy short of that. He realized early on that his best move was just to nod and say, "All right." Then he'd seek out a private moment with Rick to discuss the externalities (Hobart liked to call them), which usually meant what Angie wanted was not remotely what Angie might get.

We came in time to understand that Rick and Hobart's goal at bottom, was to simply extract an apology from Gail. Old Gail would have delivered up a sulky one for sure. It might not have satisfied, but it would have been measurably contrite. New Gail wasn't sorry for anything, in the moment or retroactively, and even once Rick (through Hobart) had offered Gail money to apologize, Gail told Hobart she might be intermittently gay but she was full-time plucky and couldn't be sorry for something she'd happily do again.

You can't call a woman a cow and then have any purchase on her, so Gail stayed firm and Angie stayed pissed while Rick, we noticed, stayed in The Anvil, and he did it alone for regular stretches, usually in daylight. Sometimes he'd get lit enough to ask for our advice, which tended to run from "Tell her to drop it" to "Put her under the breezeway". Angie would call him six or eight times an hour. We could hear his phone buzzing on the bar.

Rick from Galveston was not full-time plucky and had a substantial indecisive streak. We'd heard it from the tradesmen working up at his house, and we'd gotten a whiff of it as well from Randi. She didn't talk much about her men, probably thought the more she said the more likely we were to take the time to count them, but she did generally break us down into just two categories. There were the guys who thought they were primo, evidence be damned, and guys who knew they weren't and liked to apologize about it. Rick fell into the second slot, and all Randi would tell us about him came out sounding like general advice.

"Once you've had a go at a girl," Randi said, "she doesn't want to hear that you're sorry."

At least he was polite, clean apparently too, but even at The Anvil Rick would always eventually take one of Angie's calls and swear he was coming or going from the Tractor Supply out by the highway, and the two of them weren't even married yet.

He sure didn't fit with the Eaglesworth lineage, the way we'd come to think about it. We had that Avent and those Crawley-Lowells down as lusty scoundrels all. We couldn't say much about Frank and Adelaide and so elected not to count them, but Rick from Galveston was making his mark on the house for sure, and we felt like he had a duty to be more of a character than he was. He didn't need to be goatish but dynamic and lively would have helped.

Rick was no better than the banker sorts snatching up estates all over and then planting grapes and Christmas trees, whatever their taxes required. Naturally, we had to be stuck with a guy who wouldn't stand up to his girlfriend and marched around this world in cowboy boots.

Of course we compared him to Kandy. They'd both shown up at about the same time, and of the two of them, Kandy was the one who knew what she wanted and how to get it. We might have worried about her mess of a case, but that wasn't really on her, and she'd bulled right ahead being lesbian and had proved successful at it. Then she added to her cred one night by handling two Tylers both at once.

They were fighting, had come out of the back room of The Anvil where Randi's pool table was. They were hot with each other over money, like usual. One of them had bet the other he couldn't do something, and the other had been all in on the bet right up until he'd lost when he claimed to have been kidding all along. That was the only sort of fight those Tylers ever had.

They were logging Tylers. They worked together with a mule, and if you wanted your timber thinned and snaked, they were the ones to do it. You had to not mind them quitting at noon and never showing up on Mondays or Fridays. Somehow even their mule was lazy. If you had any fencing, he'd lean on it.

Those two had a pretty considerable history of fighting around town. They couldn't go into Cuddy's anymore or The Embers either one, and Randi would cut them off for stretches, but then they'd beg their way back in, and they were on the usual Tyler probation when they lurched out of the back room.

Randi hit them immediately with her first line of defense. She told those Tylers, "Hey!"

They do some punching, but it's rabbit punching chiefly, because they far prefer grabbing hold and jerking each other around. They'll knock over tables and irritate patrons, but people usually just let them fight until Deputy Doby shows up. He's Randi's second line, and he can often kung fu some sense into those boys.

So out they came from the back room, and most of the rest of us groaned. Randi tried her "Hey!" with the usual effect and then put in a call to the station, but Kandy had stepped in for a Corona and a Cuervo, and she wasn't about to let two grubby knuckleheads mess that up.

Kandy didn't say anything to them. She'd probably seen plenty of the Tyler variety of human in her line. Half-drunk, trashy, and completely indifferent to the norms and standards of polite society, which is essentially what lets most of us survive to see the morning. The Tyler's had no use for any of that, and if they met with cause to argue, they'd do it however they wanted wherever they were. Kandy knew you didn't talk that sort of fellow out of anything.

She left her bar stool and picked up a chair. Kandy gave it a test shake and didn't care for the heft of it. A guy sitting on a stouter one stood up and let her have his, and Kandy raised it high and put those Tylers down. When they complained and tried to get back up, she whacked them a second time.

Then Kandy gave the chair back to the man who'd been on it and was returning to her stool just as Deputy Doby came hustling in.

"What happened?" Deputy Doby asked.

"They fell over or something," Randi told him, which Doby normally wouldn't have stood for, but Randi was just unbuttoned enough to make it work.

So between Rick from Galveston and Kandy from the state police, we were with Kandy pretty much all the way, and we didn't care how many local women she found fit for purpose.

Kandy had three rounds in her that very night before she came over to see us. She never got loud or sloppy but only slightly more deliberate, as if the booze had changed her gearing and slowed her down.

"Gentlemen," she said. That's what she always said, and she usually made it sound like she very possibly meant it. "Look at something for me."

We were game, of course, and watched her pull a few snapshots out of her cargo pocket along with a little inlaid wooden box. She just set the stuff down and let us work out how we'd look at what.

Three photos. One of an old man. One a young man. One a dog. And the box had stick people on it in comically tall hats.

"Professor's uncle," Kandy told us. "That was stuff he kept. That's him old and him young. Found four pictures of that dog. What do you think about that box?"

We let Dennis take that one since he was the lone woodworker among us, even if he only made boot jacks that the shoe store people sold.

Dennis turned that box all around. It had a flat lid that slid off. "Well," he finally told Kandy, "I'd say it's kind of crap. But . . . same sort of lid as the box the toes were in."

By way of thanks (or something) Kandy told him, "Hell is truth seen too late."

Maybe Rick was right to ask. Maybe it was contagious.

FOUR

1

Ken knew the dog, so that's where we had to start. Or he felt anyway like he knew the dog. He was a big shepherd but buff-colored with speckles like he had some hound to him as well. He was a handsome boy, and in the snapshot Kandy showed us, he was standing in profile at full alert, with his ears straight up and the background sun-blasted, so it was just that dog with everything else gone white.

Ken wasn't sure for about two days because Ken's just ever so careful, and once he'd decided for certain he knew that dog, it was because he'd remembered his name

"Rollo," Ken told us. "Used to follow the boxwood guy around."

We felt like that was big news and tried to get into the annex with it, but they had the place buttoned up, and Nathan informed us through the door that Kandy was in a meeting. We figured we'd wait and went across to the cookhouse to bother

Gupta instead. He had the professor in there with him, but Dwight Remington was gone, and Gupta was using the picnic table for his lab forms and reports. He looked to be putting together the package he'd be carrying back to Richmond while the Professor came out with the odd philosophical nugget by way of support.

Gupta had a use for us and pointed at the professor. "Walk him around for a while."

We were happy enough to help and got the professor out beyond the post office before we said, "Rollo" to him about eight or fourteen times.

Roland barked. Kandy had taken her snapshot back, so we had nothing to show the professor and just kept saying, "Rollo," kept saying, "Dog."

For his part, the professor told us, "I stick my finger into existence, and it smells of nothing," and various other items in that vein. The professor tolerated us well enough, didn't seem to know the dog, and finally Edgar and Brady ganged up on Roland and convinced him to stop barking.

It turned out Kandy was tied up with the Master of Mirage and his little, round wife in the annex. She wasn't going to drive all the way up to Luray for them, but it was fine if they came to her, and she'd told them to bring their photos and any other pertinent things they had.

Because Dorcas and Johnny Wonders were both hambones at bottom, they arrived prepared to put on the show they'd done at Eaglesworth. They'd left their large props at home — the sawed lady box and the cabinet that Johnny Wonders used to step inside of and vanish — but they were ready to talk those two tricks half to death and perform most all the others.

Kandy tried to stop them, but show people are not suggestible that way, so they set up a chair for Kandy and one as well for Nathan, and then Dorcas started in with, "Imagine . . ." and went on to describe the scene.

She put them in the Eaglesworth banquet hall where they'd performed on a plank riser while looking out over the Crawley-Lowell's friends in fancy dress. Dorcas figured the crowd at about three dozen. Mostly oldsters but four or five girls, and it had made a world of difference to Dorcas' attitude to find out that dear, sweet Evelyn had actually been on the clock.

Dorcas could talk about the whole experience now and feel only moderately disgusted. The scene she'd stumbled onto no

longer spoiled the show for Dorcas, and she described the
Master of Mirage's entrance and opening feats of prestidigitation
with a fulsomeness, Kandy called it, that left her numb.

Nathan even tried to slip off, seemed frantic to have a word
with Gupta, but Kandy grabbed him by the belt and held him
fast. The Master performed his trick with brass rings and
something with face cards from a deck. They had a parakeet
instead of a dove (also instead of a bedroom shoe), and by the
time Johnny Wonders pulled it out of its empty box, he was
pretty well hitting his stride. Kandy allowed that even Nathan
had gotten into it some by then, and he fairly yelped when the
Master's walking cane turned into a clutch of flowers.

"What do you remember about the people?" Kandy asked.

Dorcas and Johnny Wonders recalled them chiefly in terms
of how pleased they'd all been with the show.

"Anybody seem off? Weird? Make a special impression?"

Between them they didn't believe so, and Dorcas said even
the men with Evelyn were both still wearing their socks. She
couldn't say why exactly, but that somehow felt courteous to her.

229

They were gathering their stuff and preparing to leave when Johnny Wonders remembered something, and he said to Dorcas, "Oh," and snapped his fingers. "Tell her about the dog."

"Right. He was sitting in a chair," Dorcas said to Kandy, and she didn't mean like curled up on the seat. "Sitting just like he'd sit on the floor only, you know, in a chair and higher."

"Big boy," Johnny Wonders said. "Every time they clapped, he barked."

Kandy had a photo for them to look at and dug it out and handed it over. "Not him, was it?"

They didn't appear to be dead certain, but they were both prepared to nod.

Those two were probably halfway to Luray before Nathan found their parakeet perched on the toilet seat.

So when we brought Ken in, it was right on time because Ken remembered Rollo, which we told Kandy about and then did what we could to help her draw Ken out.

Ken had not exactly been sitting on useful Eaglesworth information. Ever since he'd seen the snapshot of himself in the striped shirt he'd loved, Ken had been trying to dredge up pertinent memories from that time and couldn't. A chunk of his life seemed to be closed off from him.

"I had a sled," Ken had told us one night at The Anvil, "and then I had a bike. A couple of years apart I'm pretty sure, but I can't picture any of it."

We didn't know what to do to help him. We don't have an actual therapist around. We had a man a few years back who did some marriage counseling and taught yoga, but it turned out he was dodging a warrant in Nevada where he'd fleeced a payday loan outfit that he'd been working for. The only folks we knew who'd hired him for counseling were married now to other people, but Lacy who works in the Baptist church took his yoga class and hasn't been down with sciatica ever since.

All we knew of his technique was that he often said, "Let's be still," so what we had for Ken was something from a Nevada fraudster that we inflicted on him like you'd toss rocks at a cow.

"Jesus, boys," Ken finally told us. "I'm as still as I'm going to get."

It was maybe two days later when Ken had his big breakthrough. Ken started recalling his life between the sled and the bicycle, and he boiled it all down for us, told us, "Keith."

Keith was Ken's mother's sister's boy. He was two years older than Ken, and they'd been tight and had roamed together as children. As a grown-up, Keith had lived one of those lives folks around him couldn't really explain. Stretches of ordinary with eruptions in between when Keith would blow up a job or throw over a girlfriend or get himself arrested, and none of it would ever seem to have been caused by anything beyond Keith's need to have a spasm and turn his stuff all upside down.

His mother had him scanned and tested and tried to get him help, but whatever Keith had no doctor could detect.

"Died, didn't he?" Edgar asked Ken.

He shook his head and said back, "Worse."

Ken's cousin Keith was doing double life in Wallens Ridge Penitentiary. "He got in with some boys on some kind of job, and one of them shot some people." That was how Ken told it, but when Kandy started nailing details down, we found out they'd brought Keith in as a wheelman when the guy they'd been intending to use wrecked his car. Keith was in one of his quiet spells, was working down near Roanoke delivering shop towels and rubber floor mats in a van.

He knew one of the stick-up boys from a bar he used to go to, and once Keith had been looped in on the heist, he could either drive or die. People got shot and, the way it works, they all pulled the trigger, and with his record, Keith had hit habitual offender anyway. So he was sitting down by Big Stone Gap with all the other lifers.

"If I go all the way down there," Kandy asked Ken, "what's he going to say?"

"I think," Ken said, "he'll tell you all about the boxwood guy."

Kandy had a couple of photos of the professor's Uncle Sanford, and she showed them to Ken. The geezer pic was only two years old. A man in a housecoat was getting fed a chunk of birthday cake by a tiny black woman wearing green surgical scrubs. His thin, gray hair was standing straight up, and he had one chalky hand raised. He could have been any old white guy getting force fed his dessert.

Then she gave Ken the older photo, and Ken knew just where he was with that.

"That's him," Ken said. "He did everything up there."

Kandy let us sit by while she talked to Ken. She'd brought us all into the annex where she couldn't altogether prevent us from seeing the stuff they'd taped to the walls. Photos and police reports and property plats and maps along with note pages and newsprint taken out of Adelaide's journal.

We kept trying to move in and read it all, but Kandy would just tell us, "Uh uh."

At first, we thought she was afraid we'd piece together some mystery she'd cracked open, but Kandy straightened us out pretty quick on that. "You don't know what you're looking at," she said.

In the end, that's probably a far more useful mantra than "Let's be still". If we were to learn anything at all from our Eaglesworth affair, it was probably that we never quite know what we're looking at in the end.

Ken's Uncle Sandy info turned out to be almost exclusively second hand. He'd blocked out that patch of time between his sled and his bicycle because Keith, his cousin, had kind of blocked it out as well. Ken seemed to have something on the order of sympathetic amnesia.

"Keith got tangled up with Sandy," Ken said. "I was just kind of around."

We'd made a promise not to chime in while Kandy was talking to Ken, and all of us kept it but, of course, for Roland who got put out into the annex lot because Kandy wasn't kidding.

Kandy then led Ken across the Eaglesworth grounds as he could conjure them from that time, and Ken remembered the hawks in the poplar grove and the smell of the Temple of Luxor, a powerful blend of pulpwood and rot. He'd been all through the boxwood maze and told Kandy, "We went up there whenever we wanted." The reason being that Sandy the groundsman had a special fondness for children and the Crawley-Lowells didn't care what he did since they were almost always drunk.

We were aware there were grownups around, especially in books and on TV, who did all sorts of evil things to kids, and maybe because the Crawley-Lowells were loaded and inattentive, they could well have given this Sandy the space and leisure to be that kind of man.

That's what we suspected we were looking at, and we thought maybe Ken had walked in on it like Johnny Wonders' little, round wife, and Ken decided to have a blank spot between his sled and his bike after that.

"You sure this guy's dead?" Edgar asked Kandy and then joined Roland out in the parking lot.

"Still in touch with your cousin?"

Ken shook his head.

"Want to go with me to see him?"

Ken went, of course, notwithstanding that what he told Kandy back was, "No."

Kandy also took Gupta. It was his last favor to her before he returned to Richmond, and she wanted to make the trip in his sedan. Kandy imagined she might need help keeping Ken steady and calm, but Ken's the sort who, when he gets anxious, withdraws and shuts on down. Mostly Gupta told Ken stories about growing up in the Brushy Mountains with a father from Pipe Stem, West Virginia, and a mother from Kerala. He ate better than most hillbillies but got beat up for being brown.

It's a long pull down to Wallens Ridge, precisely the spot you'd stick a crew you didn't want to see again. They took the interstate south just a mile or two from the Tennessee border and then turned west out towards Gate City and climbed a ridge on Route 23. Then they dropped into the gap and drove out to where the road quit. Razor wire. Guard towers. Slits instead of windows. Ancient hardwood mountain forest all around.

A state police badge didn't pull much weight at Wallens Ridge, and Keith's unit was in a partial shutdown due to some inmate mischief, the kind that probably happens at a place like that six or seven times a day. So they waited in a big gray room perched on creaky plastic chairs, and the way we heard it, Kandy took it for about an hour and then she pulled aside a guard and gave him just the right amount of grief.

He took them back to another gray room, and after a little while more Keith's cousin came in. They'd left him shackled. There was no fixing that, and they all sat around a table. The meeting opened with a kind of reunion, which would be Ken and Keith both saying, "Hey."

Kandy pulled out her notebook, and Keith informed her, "I'll need five hundred in canteen money."

Kandy told him, "Seventy-five."

And Keith said, "What are we here for?"

"Remember Rollo?" his cousin asked him. "Big dog up on he hill?"

"I guess I do." Keith tugged up his jumpsuit leg and showed off a scar. "Took his bone. Wished I hadn't."

"And Sandy?" Ken again.

That only rated a nod.

"They'll be wanting to see your feet."

"Two hundred."

Kandy waited until Keith had kicked off his sneakers before she nodded. He put both of his pale feet on the tabletop. The left one was missing its little toe.

"What happened?" Kandy asked.

"Fooling around with some loppers. What are y'all into?"

"Sandy's dead," Ken told his cousin. "So it's all right to say what he did."

"He didn't do nothing to me."

"I remember it different," Ken told him.

"You was like seven years old or something. What the hell you know?" Keith shook his head and snorted, said again with some defiance, "He didn't do nothing to me."

Keith put his feet back onto the floor and shifted so that his shackles clanked and rattled. Nobody said anything for a couple of minutes, and then Keith volunteered, "I used to help him cut bushes." He glanced at his bare foot. "He liked being friendly. You know how that goes sometimes."

Kandy jotted in her ratty notebook. "Didn't his wife drown or something?"

"His little girl," Keith told her. "Rip tide's a hell of a thing."

Kandy kept Ken from talking, and they all just sat there waiting.

"Connie," Keith said eventually. "By the time she washed up, the turtles and fish had been at her pretty good."

"They'll do that," Kandy allowed.

"He used to give us fireballs, remember?" Ken said.

"You maybe." Keith grunted. "Used to give me . . . other stuff."

Then Keith grabbed his shoes, yelled for the guard, and said Kandy's way, "Two hundred." It was a pleading reminder dressed up like a threat.

They stopped in a Mexican joint in Big Stone Gap because there wasn't a Hardee's around, and Kandy stayed outside for the first little while giving instructions to Nathan on the phone so he could do further digging on Uncle Sandy and find out about the daughter while they were making the long drive home.

Inside Gupta was pushing around a tamale while entertaining the odd comment from Ken.

"How does somebody like that decide," Ken asked, "who he likes and who he doesn't?"

"Just like the rest of us probably. I thought this was some kind of taco. What did you get?"

Ken tilted his plate Gupta's way as he told him, "This."

Once Kandy had come in, Ken wondered her way how somebody like Uncle Sandy figured out who his favorites would be.

"Rather have nine toes?" Kandy asked him, "and whatever else came with it?" It wasn't tough love exactly, but it was a long way from "let's be still".

The way we heard it, Ken never quite settled down or clammed up on the ride back up but kept telling Kandy and Gupta what he was remembering at last. Ken back then had followed his cousin Keith most everywhere, and that meant near-daily visits to Eaglesworth.

"That dog was theirs, but they didn't have time for it."

"The Crawley-Lowells?" Kandy asked him.

Ken nodded. "They didn't know how to do anything. Couldn't drive a nail, couldn't cook and, by the looks of them, stayed too drunk to even figure out what to wear. She'd come out in this long white thing you could see straight through, and he'd go around in his underpants. We'd see both of them peeing in the yard." After a bit, Ken added, "Keith wouldn't let me cut the bushes."

"Good on him," Kandy said.

Ken by then had remembered enough to nod and tell her, "Yeah."

~~~~~~

We'd been minding the professor all the while, of course, and when it got late and they hadn't come back, Brady ended up taking him home. Brady had married one of those women who thinks she's Christian and charitable until the good works hit the pavement when she's usually just flinty and mean. So she was all for the professor coming with Brady until that's what actually happened.

It wasn't like she had to feed Reginald Duff. We'd filled him up with chicken pot pie and succotash over at Cuddy's, and we'd taken him, of course, for a nightcap at The Anvil.

Karen, Brady's wife, has stout objections to hair. That's why they've not had a pet or children or awfully many friends because pets and people tend to be fur-bearing, and Karen can barely tolerate what drops off of her.

"Police work, you know?" Brady said to his wife once he'd ushered the professor inside. "We're doing some good here," he told her, and while she failed to bolt for the Dustbuster, she asked Brady to take the professor into the den where she keeps a top sheet on the sofa.

By way of hello and thank you, Reginald Duff said to her, "We meet only those who already exist in our subconscious."

So the professor sat on a sofa with a flat sheet underneath him while Brady, off in the kitchen, got hissed at by his wife who objected to the professor on the grounds that he was bushy and stank of drink. Brady was moderately bushy and, of course, stank of drink himself, so she was very likely twice as mad as normal, which didn't keep her from smiling at Reginald Duff and offering him mints she'd pulled, and he proved happy to stick his paw in the bowl and take just about all of them.

They had a guest room with a twin bed and a stationary bike and an ironing board in it, and Brady gave the professor a towel and bid the man good night. He didn't get a particularly memorable snatch of philosophy back.

"Sounded about half Latin," Brady told us once we saw him the following morning.

The trouble was that, come dawn, Brady found a made bed and a towel but no sign of the professor anywhere.

2

To her credit, it was Angie who decided on the party. Rick was adequately sick of us to be tepid to the thing, but Angie seemed to recognize that house meant something to us since we'd been down on the low ground looking up at it for years. They set it up for a Saturday, two to five, and on the notices Angie scattered around with a sketch of Eaglesworth on it, she made sure we understood that she meant five o'clock sharp. "No Lingerers!!!" is what she said.

The painting took longer than expected since they kept changing their minds, and they had a percolation problem with the drain field because the soil up there was red clay, but the place looked little short of spectacular from down at the road, especially once they'd spread a few fresh inches of pea gravel on the drive.

We hated the professor wouldn't be around for the party, but we flat couldn't find him. Kandy and Glenn put out all the bulletins on the man that they could manage, but for a big hairy guy in a fuzzy tweed suit and yellow flip-flops who was likely as not to talk to you in Schopenhauer and Kant, he didn't leave any trace beyond maybe a foxhound's worth of hair over at Brady and Karen's house.

We'd pumped Ken about his visit to Wallens Ridge and what had passed between him and his cousin, but it seems he had used up most of his commentary in the car on the way back home. He told us he'd let Kandy work out what she wanted to make of it, and we were afraid she might just keep that to herself.

So we had concerns and anxiety but figured a house party couldn't hurt, and everybody showed up at two on the dot, and by God we all lingered like crazy. Angie was still trying to drive us off at half-past six. She called the law even though Glenn and Rachel were up there with us. Kandy was working on ski do man's sister who'd not wanted or intended to come but had brought her brother once his starter had locked up.

We all got to find out that Rick from Galveston's girlfriend thought we were vulgar and boorish because she had quite a lot to say on that front from about five thirty on. Eventually, of course, we made Angie cry, but they were tears of profane rage, so there was entertainment value in lingering even longer, and Rick had gotten so full of bourbon he actually encouraged us to stay.

At least we were out of the house and in the yard where Ken opened up ever so slightly about his visit to the prison down at Wallens Ridge, and then he showed us all where he'd seen the Crawley-Lowells pee.

Rick gave semi-sober tours of the interior for a while, and it was quite a thing to see Eaglesworth in near pristine condition after the rats and the mold and the vandals and the many years of neglect. The place was grand again and smelled of paint and varnish and echoed like a cavern because there were only a couple of chairs inside, and they were the thrift store dinette variety. When people tried to talk to Rick about how he'd furnish the place, he wouldn't say much of anything beyond some version of "we'll see".

Looking back, that was a stone-cold clue they had something else in mind, and it could be Rick had spent so lavishly that he needed to recoup and simply couldn't afford to both fix the house and have it. For all we knew, he was still sitting on his property in Texas while his girlfriend plainly didn't care for being up amongst us at all.

Worse still for Rick, Angie got some stink somehow off of Randi. Randi had taken off from The Anvil long enough to get an Eaglesworth tour from Rick. He walked her around the property and all up through the house while Angie made a show in the yard of wondering where those two could be.

Then Rick and Randi came out of the house, and Randi had her hand on Rick's arm. That tore it for Angie. She marched straight over to them where she had sharp words for her boyfriend and sharper ones for the half-unbuttoned woman he was with.

Then Randi joined us briefly and accepted from Edgar a slug from his bottle of rye while we all watched Angie go true bill (we had to think) on Rick's ass for a bit.

"She seems nice," Randi told us, and since she'd done what she needed, she left.

You don't put a place like Eaglesworth on the regular real estate market. You don't run a photo of it with all the other McMansions on offer or stick a sign out in the yard. You don't want ordinary people coming to see it just because they can, so

Rick took on a swanky realtor from up around D.C. who printed up an Eaglesworth brochure on something approaching cardstock, and he put it in the hands of certain vetted clients and well-heeled friends of friends, the sort of people who would have likely preferred Jeffersonian digs but were willing to make a few minor allowances.

These folks would roll up in the realtor's Range Rover for their discrete Eaglesworth showings, and the enterprise stayed so low-key we didn't know it was going on.

The county inspector who did the last walk through after every scrap of work was finally finished happened to be making some notes in his truck when a house-hunting couple showed up. That guy knew a realtor when he saw one, even a realtor with French cuffs and an unvented blazer and the sort of suede loafers you'd never wear to find a property line. Then that inspector had lunch at Cuddy's, and word got out the place was for sale.

By the time we were fully clued in, Rick already had three offers, and those buyers competed with each other until the winner overpaid. Rick had gotten the house for the price of a tax lien and sold it for nearly seven million when he would have quite happily taken three or four. So he suddenly had enough for a fine Galveston condo on the actual water.

Rick and Angie packed up their necessaries in Angie's German coupe, which included Gruber the three-legged cat and ill-humored, half-blind Carlton, and Rick gave his dinette chairs and air mattress to the boy who was cutting his lawn.

He didn't say goodbye to any of us. Angie, of course, never would, but we felt like we rated a shout and a wave from Rick. The last words from him to anybody around went to the boy with the mower.

"That mattress," Rick informed him, "kind of leaks."

Nobody moved in for many weeks. You don't buy estates because you need them, and even after two trucks had rolled up and gotten emptied through the front door, the place just sat for another month with both the porch lamps burning. Then a man came and re-welded the gate down by the road so it would shut and lock.

We heard from Rachel who got it from Glenn that Kandy was writing some kind of report, and Glenn felt confident that he'd be copied on it, that it wouldn't simply go straight to Richmond with Kandy following close behind. She was clearly up to something because we didn't see much of her, and we had a bucket of questions we wanted to ask.

The one solid good thing we had going on was progress on our plaque. We'd swallowed hard finally and roped in the historical society ladies. They knew who in Richmond to touch for favors and how best to lobby for the thing.

Our crew started out with firm ideas on what our plaque should say, but dealing with those ladies served to wear us down, and it got where to we yielded the thrust of the project largely to them provided our finished plaque didn't mention Jamestown once.

A woman eventually came from whatever arm of the government deals with roadside historical markers. There were signage placement considerations and prose strategies to weigh, which we left to the historical society ladies who fed the woman lunch and then took her as close to Eaglesworth as they could get with the gate locked tight.

They found a spot they all liked for our plaque, about twenty yards east of the driveway, and our campaign to eclipse Longstreet's retreat came to its happy end with four women on he shoulder dodging traffic and shaking hands.

Then the state had to manufacture the thing which, according to folks in Richmond, would probably take them just south of forever. The older you get, the more success has a way of looking like that.

Happily, Kandy found Professor Reginald Duff. Actually, thirty-eight students found him when he showed up back at the Christian Science college and tried to teach them about the tenants of German idealism in their geology class.

Dr. Pike called Kandy and told her all about it, and we were happy to learn the professor had made it all the way back to the valley. Dr. Pike told Kandy that Reginald Duff had a head doctor over there who'd dealt with the professor through the years and knew how to tune him up.

"You might have told me that sooner," Kandy said to him.

Dr. Pike responded with a couplet. He then asked, "Your case — sovitur?" That allowed him to explain to Kandy that he was using the Latin for 'solved'.

Kandy gave him something back that was French Canadian for hosehead.

Then she dropped by The Anvil to tell us all the professor was home and fine, which gave Randi the chance to talk to

Kandy about the cabinet maker's sister because Kandy had

dropped Randi, and Randi couldn't quite live with that.

~~~~~~

Kandy might have been a young woman still, but she'd

already rubbed against a wealth of warped and devious people.

Not that she'd personally chased them down as an officer of the

state police, but she'd assisted her veteran colleagues on any

number of ghastly cases and so had read the files and seen the

photos and was aware in a detailed way of what humans can

sometimes get up to with each other.

She'd helped with arrests and had watched interrogations,

had sat in courtrooms and heard detailed descriptions of

wickedness.

Long before she'd reached us, Kandy had developed a

decided opinion about people. "Some of them," we'd heard her

say, "just aren't any good."

While we were never permitted to read her report, Kandy

aid the nut of it out in The Anvil. She'd posted a notice around town by way of calling a general meeting, and even a few of our teetotalers showed up. The state police paid for the first round, which kicked the thing off right.

Even Nathan came, and we felt certain he'd never been in a bar before because the light in such places was poor enough to hide a world of filth. At least in The Anvil you got Randi half unbuttoned, and Nathan appeared to appreciate that.

Kandy had brought along evidence and photographs, a couple of lab reports, which she let us know we'd be free to look at once she'd talked stuff through. Kandy was just about to start when the Master of Mirage and his little, round wife came in. They were dressed for a show — his suit too big and her spangly gown way too little — and Kandy told us, "Thought you might need a little magic after this."

"Let's start with some actual history," Kandy said and then brought up Joyce, the historical society lady most at home in front of a crowd. Of the remaining two, one of them could only talk if she was reading notecards, and the other one tended to get unduly anxious and stutter and sweat.

So it was Joyce who brought the Avents over into the Chesapeake Bay, and she told us what that first batch would have seen if they'd arrived, say, on the Godspeed, which naturally led to the Jamestown colony. That's about when Kandy said, "Nope," and shook her head.

Joyce moved on to our Avent, Caleb, who had two bookworms for brothers while he preferred the woods and started a business cooking turpentine. Then she leapt ahead to Caleb's first bride (fresh in from Kinvara). We got way too much about the lives of her people back on Galway Bay, and Kandy eventually made a noise in her neck, which proved sufficient for Joyce who talked about the marriage getting consecrated and then dissolving while avoiding the salty details, so folks shouted out a few.

Somebody mentioned that Avent's love of sherry, and a lady across the way we didn't really know said she knew for a fact our Avent had killed a neighbor over a hound.

Caleb Avent died of an infection. Joyce told us precisely which one and listed all the symptoms. Then she lingered over the damage done when the house was abandoned to the weather while our dead Avent's bookworm brothers failed to maintain Eaglesworth.

Joyce told us the Crawleys had piled up money with slag pits and regional rail lines while the Lowells had long been sitting on a textile fortune.

"Our two," Joyce assured us, "were not best of breed."

Kandy had Crawley-Lowell era photographs that she and Nathan had collected, some of people and some of the estate and some of just the countryside around. She divvied them up and handed them out while Joyce proposed those two had made our Avent seem genteel.

Joyce didn't care for the Crawley-Lowells. We could tell that well enough. They had paid for some high-school sports equipment and had helped the Presbyterians when a freak windstorm took their steeple down. They'd also put Eaglesworth on the garden club tour for about a half dozen years until a fanatic helped herself to a potted fern in the conservatory. They'd pretty much kept the gate shut after that.

Mr. Crawley died in his sleep. He'd been unwell for some months according to Joyce who walked us through his assorted infirmities, and then she and the other two ladies gave us a decent quarter hour on Hudson the manservant and the boarding house years. Because they couldn't help themselves, that included a fair few minutes on the type of pistol Mrs. Crawley-Lowell used to fire into the air. A Mauser C96 that chambered 9mm rounds.

After that, Joyce yielded to Kandy to speak to us about what Joyce called "unfortunate paraphilia". She said it with a tortured grimace and a full-body shiver like you might get from a Jamestown puritan lass with a quartet of cue balls to drop.

"All right," Kandy told us by way of preamble and then started in with what she'd found out about the Crawley-Lowells. She didn't sugarcoat any of it or fuzz it up with jargon. They'd been people with money who'd liked what they'd liked, and they'd bought it wherever they could.

Kandy was more interested in their gardener and all-purpose groundsman. "Sanford Tyler Royce," she told us and showed us two pictures of him — as a young man fresh out of the service with an angry scar on his chin and as an old guy with his thin hair standing up.

A woman spoke up, told Kandy her daddy had sold Sanford Royce manure. "Used to make me go in the house," she said, "when he'd come out with his truck."

"He ever tell you why?" Kandy asked her.

He hadn't. Nobody likely would have. You dodged trouble as you met it in those days and protected what you could, but you didn't get into people's business or try to remedy anything. We'd had nuts wandering loose all over the landscape back then.

"He probably felt protected up there," Kandy told us of Uncle Sandy. "Chances seem good he had stuff on the Crawley-Lowells, like who was dead under the breezeway and who was buying sex from schoolgirls. Power's a funny thing," Kandy added, "because of how it shifts."

"What did he do?" Edgar asked. "He the toe box guy?"

"Sanford Royce lost his daughter," Kandy said, "and that could have been what broke him. I think we can say he took liberties with some kids up there, and from what I can tell, the toes are probably the least of it."

We wanted chapter and verse from Kandy and yet weren't eager to come near it. It was like we were craving details and blind ignorance both at once.

"You might be acquainted with a few of these kids," Kandy said and then paused to have a look at us. "Might even be one or two of them in here." She stopped talking again for a moment "You can't hurt a child without hurting everybody he'll ever know. If this town comes away with nothing else, come away with that."

We suddenly found we couldn't help but look at us as well.

"There's nothing more I can do," Kandy told us. "There's nobody to do it to, and all the digging in the world won't help."

A few folks grumbled. They felt like Kandy's duty was to file some charges on somebody somehow, but that was the minority view.

"It's ok," she told us, "to be sorry Sanford Royce could just die once."

Of course there were questions for Kandy, and they were chiefly about the toes. How did they come to be in that box? What had they been nipped with? What was the story with all those snapshots stuck back in the walls? And who'd throw a party and end up sticking a dead guest under the breezeway? While nobody asked about curly maple, the historical society ladies were pleased to inform the gathering at large that it was prized by artisans and was also known as fiddleback and sometimes tiger stripe.

Then Kandy cut us off. She told us this world's packed full of stuff not worth knowing. Once we'd quieted down, she introduced the Master of Mirage. His opening patter was about as musty and moth-eaten as his suit, and the crowd generally seemed inclined to doubt we needed a magic show.

The mere fact that we were having one set us wondering about Kandy's judgment, but then the Master of Mirage connected solid brass rings by tapping them together, turned a walking stick into a bouquet of flowers, brought a lady up to eagle eye him as he made a matchbox disappear and then caused it to show back up again with her wedding band inside it. That lady couldn't help herself. That lady had to shriek.

He had us from then on out, and we were doing some shrieking too by the time he plucked a calico kitten from his empty hat and made a gin and tonic vanish. In the wake of theatrical gestures and a cloud of cracker ball smoke, Johnny Wonders simply picked up the glass and drained it.

As the years go by, it's easy to forget that you can be delighted, and we like to think Kandy was out to remind us all as best she could.

3

We never knew the people who bought Eaglesworth. They rarely came into town. They'd drive down from D.C. with all the food and stuff they needed, and they'd stay up on the hill for a night or three and then drive back. Occasionally, friends would join them. We'd see the cars come and go. We'd spy children sometimes and a dog or two in the yard, but it wasn't like you were going to run into any of that crowd in Dooley's or the Kroger. They bought better stuff up in the city and hauled it down.

We also never gave Kandy a proper goodbye. She gave us one, but we didn't know it. A few days after the magic show, Kandy popped into The Anvil. She had her usual beer and a bump and a quick chat with Randi at the bar. Then she said back our way, "Gentlemen," saluted us, and left.

We took it to mean she was only off to the Laurel Lodge for the evening, but when Kandy's dirty green Ford passed through town early the next morning, it didn't pull in at the annex but just kept going east towards Richmond. It took us three or four days to quit expecting to see her at Cuddy's and around.

Ken became more forceful after Kandy left and infinitely more chatty, and we discovered we'd chiefly liked him because he didn't say much at all. Then Joyce set Ken up with one of the other historical society ladies — the sweaty one — and they so hit it off that we lost him to culture and to taste.

We talked about driving to the valley and paying a call on the professor, but we also talked about going fishing out in Idaho.

Our plaque wasn't what we'd hoped for. It was silver and black like all the others, and they'd etched a likeness of our Avent's face up near the top. He was a beard and a hat with eyes in between, and he was standing next to a pine tree with a bucket hanging from it. In the paragraph underneath, we got a lot about turpentine and then brief mention of Eaglesworth and the year our Avent died. It was better than Longstreet's throttled army, but not by awfully much.

The people who owned the house complained our plaque blinded them to traffic. That's what their lawyer's letter told us anyway, so the boys from VDOT came out and moved the thing across the road where the kudzu soon enough started easing up the post.

It got to where Eaglesworth was back to sitting empty most of the time. The people who'd bought it had other houses and plenty of spots to visit, and maybe they figured they'd use it in coming years but just leave it to languish first. Of course, people got in like people will, and they plundered and they pilfered. Deputy Doby caught a boy coming down one night with a truck full of copper downspouts and brass kick plates he'd pried off the doors.

By then our plaque was so kudzued over you couldn't hope to read it, and we'd ride through between that lump in the vines and that empty house on the hilltop and try to imagine what the professor might tell us after all we'd seen. Possibly "Change is the only permanent thing," or "In order for a light to shine brightly, darkness must be present," or maybe he'd go with something like "Hope is a waking dream."

Manufactured by Amazon.ca
Bolton, ON